ADVENTURES OF AN ELEPHANT BOY

Also by Leonard Wibberley

Stranger At Killknock
The Quest of Excalibur
Beware of the Mouse
Take Me to Your President
McGillicuddy McGotham
The Mouse That Roared

Mrs. Searwood's Secret Weapon
The Mouse on the Moon
A Feast of Freedom
The Island of the Angels
The Hands of Cormac Joyce
The Road from Toomi

NONFICTION

Yesterday's Land
Towards a Distant Island

No Garlic in the Soup
The Land That Isn't There

JUVENILES (Fiction)

Peter Treegate's War
Kevin O'Connor and the Light Brigade
The Wound of Peter Wayne

John Treegate's Musket
Peter Treegate's War
Sea Captain from Salem

JUVENILES (Nonfiction)

Wes Powell—Conqueror of the Colorado
The Life of Winston Churchill

John Barry—Father of the Navy
The Epics of Everest

ADVENTURES OF AN *Elephant Boy*

by Leonard Wibberley

WILLIAM MORROW & COMPANY, INC.

NEW YORK 1968

To Voltaire—may he live forever.

Chapter
One

WHEN Dr. Pangloss became President of the
Best of All Possible Nations (an event which in no way
surprised him for he believed that in the best of all
possible worlds it was inevitable that the best of all
possible people should become the president of the
Best of All Possible Nations) he sent to Asia for an
elephant boy.

"It is manifestly necessary that I explain to the emerging peoples of the East how matters are handled in this
Best of All Possible Nations, and it follows from this as
two follows from one that I should bring an elephant
boy to this country as my personal guest and show him
how every citizen is able to pursue his own personal
quest for life, liberty and happiness," he said.

Everybody agreed that in this matter President Pangloss was certainly proceeding with that faith and belief
in the common people which had—a few other trifles
being added—secured him the election, and only a
highly placed general of the Army bothered to inquire

from what country of Asia Pangloss was going to get his elephant boy.

"It doesn't matter," said the President, "so long as he is a representative of the common people of the Eastern world which we are trying to reach while they emerge."

"If it doesn't matter," said the general, "get him from India. We are reliably informed that the democratic way of life is being threatened in other places where they have elephant boys. A few Army advisers have been sent to them and the bombing should commence shortly."

So it was that Hari Ranjit Singh, quietly watering his elephant, Golden Lotus, on the banks of a tributary of the Ganges, was one evening approached by two men with close-cropped hair, wearing charcoal gray flannel suits and sweating rather heavily.

"We have been sent to bring you to the Best of All Possible Nations as the personal guest of Dr. Pangloss, our President," said one of them. "Come down off that elephant so that you can be fingerprinted, photographed, given shots for smallpox, tetanus, typhoid, diphtheria, polio, influenza, syphilis, gonorrhea, measles and writer's palsy. Also deloused and a security check run on you."

"I am quite well," said Hari Ranjit Singh. "And I believe that I already live in the best of all possible nations. Here, in the evening Golden Lotus and I bathe with pleasure, sharing the joy of the water and at times the patter of the rain in the mango leaves, or the rustling of the wind through the tamarinds; and, trusting and loving each other, we wish to go nowhere else."

8

"That river is full of bugs," said one of the men. "Keep bathing in it and you will not live to be forty. And that elephant probably has intestinal parasites. It would certainly have to be quarantined, so you cannot bring it with you."

"We are offering you an opportunity of escaping from the ignorance and superstitions which have kept your people enslaved for three thousand years," said the other man. "So come off that elephant and be fingerprinted and get your shots."

Hari Ranjit Singh still had no desire to leave his amiable elephant and the gentle river, but he had been brought up in ignorance to believe all that he was told, to be polite to strangers and never to be so discourteous as to turn down proffered hospitality. So he bade an affectionate good-bye to Golden Lotus and was given a little while to take leave of his family, including his father and his mother, his sisters and their husbands, his brothers and their wives, his sisters' husbands' sisters and brothers and his brothers' wives' brothers and sisters and his sisters' husbands' sisters and brothers' children and the same on his brothers' side. Of course he had not time to say good-bye personally to all these because President Pangloss' men were in a hurry to get him to a big city where the rites necessary to his admission to the Best of All Possible Nations, similar to the rites required for admission to Paradise in some religions, would be administered.

"You must be glad at least to get away from that howling pack of relatives," said one of the men when at last they got into the big car in which they were to

9

travel to the city, Hari's mother meanwhile giving him a freshly made *roti* for the journey.

"Howling pack of relatives?" said Hari. "Whatever do you mean? They are all of the same blood as I and so I live in them and they live in me. Surely matters are the same in the Best of All Possible Nations."

"Far from it," said the other man, whose name was Bud (his companion's name was Sam). "But we have a special day on which we love our mothers."

"And another one for loving our fathers," said Sam. "Don't forget Father's Day."

"One day?" cried Hari. "Don't you send them necklets of flowers, and pieces of roast goat meat, and bread dough and herbs and such things every day?"

"Certainly not," said Sam and Bud together. "How can you do things like that and keep in touch with the stock market? First things first. But we are the only nation in the world that has a Father's Day and a Mother's Day, and don't you forget it."

The drive to the city was a long one, and when the sun was about to set Hari begged his two companions to stop the car for a moment. This they agreed to do, thinking that he wished to relieve himself, which certainly was the case with them. They therefore retired discreetly to a bush and did what was necessary but when they returned it was to see Hari prostrating himself in the road with great reverence in the direction of Mecca.

"If I'd known he just wanted to pray and not take a leak I wouldn't have stopped the car," said Sam. "We're late already."

However, toleration of the religion of others being

10

part of the law of the Best of All Possible Nations, Bud and Sam permitted Hari to finish his prayers though they could scarcely conceal a certain contempt for the manner of them, bowing as he had done in the middle of the road and utterly prostrating himself in the humblest manner for all to see.

"Were you praying for anything special?" asked Bud.

"To worship God as I am commanded and also to ask of Him a great favor."

"What kind of a favor?" asked Sam.

"That He will graciously permit Golden Lotus to have a calf," said Hari. "That would bring the greatest joy to me and to her."

"Your God is interested in that elephant?" said Sam with a wink at his companion.

"Certainly He is since He created her," said Hari.

This reply seemed to the two of them so simpleminded that they made no comment on it, contenting themselves with an exchange of glances which indicated that they considered they were in the company of a fool of remarkable ignorance. They questioned him a little, however, for lack of any other topic of conversation, about his religious beliefs and could not refrain from saying that they held many of his religious practices absurd.

"It is plainly very stupid to have to bow to a city and say prayers at certain hours of the day," said Bud. "And not drinking any alcohol is pure nonsense. No man of any intelligence could submit to that kind of a rule. How can you continue in a religion that is so harsh and so unreasonable?"

"Your question surprises me," said Hari. "Surely in

your country religion is not designed to please man but rather to worship God? You cannot have fallen into the error of pleasing yourselves in your religious practices and ignoring God."

"In our country," said Bud, "we have freedom of conscience."

"It's a part of the democratic process," said Sam. "About which," he added, "you plainly have a lot to learn. Every man worships God as he wishes and nothing else will suit us."

"But if that is the case," cried Hari, "then every man makes his own god and God is not God, but is only something that is made by those who worship Him."

"No," said Bud. "We believe that God speaks to each man and tells each man what he is to do to serve God. We call that conscience."

"That is very remarkable," said Hari. "Tell me, how many people are there in your country?"

"About two hundred million," said Sam.

"Then it is possible that there would be two hundred million ways of worshiping God or—to put the matter another way around—that each of these two hundred million people could decide that God wanted to be worshiped in a manner different from the rest of the two hundred million."

"Perfectly correct," said Bud. "Freedom of conscience."

"God then, in your view, is part of the democratic process," said Hari. "I do not wish to be rude, but I would not like such a god and I could not worship him. If He is to be God at all, he must be superior to

12

man, and He must himself say how He is to be worshiped."

"Religion has to change with the times," said Sam. "All that kneeling stuff is out. We used to kneel in our churches once, like you did in the middle of the road, but now we sit. And the pews are more comfortable."

"Yes," said Hari. "But I think that is not what God told man to do but what man decided to do for his own comfort. Would you like to have a piece of the *roti* my mother made for me?"

"What's it got in it?" asked Bud.

"It is dough made from water and flour and without any fat, and inside are chopped mangoes and tamarind rinds and a little curry powder and boiled goat meat."

"Goat meat?" exclaimed Bud. "I'd rather starve than eat goat meat." But a little while later he was engaged in a discussion with Sam on the stupidity of the people of India who would rather starve than eat cow's meat.

Before they got to the city, Hari learned that his two companions belonged to an organization called the Secret Service, part of whose duties it was to guard President Pangloss from assassins.

"Do you mean that the President of the Best of All Possible Nations is in danger from murderers?" exclaimed Hari in surprise.

"About once in every sixty years on an average one of them is assassinated," said Bud. "The assassination rate is between eight and nine percent. Somewhat higher than Russian tsars. But if you count attempts at assassination, I suppose they would amount to one attempt in every four years."

13

"How can that be in such a country?" demanded Hari. "Surely you are inventing tales for your own amusement?"

"No," said Sam. "It's the truth. You see, the President has more power than any other person on earth. He has more power even than any king in the world."

"But is not your nation a democracy?" asked Hari.

"I think we ought to get a little rest while we can," said Bud. "You will have plenty of time to find out everything when you get there."

Chapter Two

THE following day, having spent the night alone in a very large room of a hotel (he had never slept alone in all his life but always in a room with many others, this producing a sense of both security and happiness), Hari Ranjit Singh was subjected to those rites necessary to gain entrance to the Best of All Possible Nations.

A swarm of men invaded his room before he was out of bed and battened upon him. They took blood in small amounts from the tips of his fingers and in larger amounts from a vein in his arm. They opened his mouth and probed at his teeth and at his tongue, which they pushed down with a pieec of flat wood in order to see into his stomach. They shined a bright light into his eyes and also into his ears. They hit him on the knees with a rubber hammer, made him cough, made him say certain mystic syllables while they put their instruments on his chest and on his back, thumped him lightly with their fingers, pinched the

15

nails of his hands, made him urinate in one jar and spit in another, stood him facing a wall while they made him draw in his breath and hold it, meanwhile aiming some deadly ray at his back. They made him lie down while they pulled his legs and twisted them to the right and the left. In short they submitted his person to every invasion and outrage imaginable, at the same time hardly saying a word but to do this or do that. Then they left him, talking with some animation among themselves but telling him nothing.

Scarcely had one group left than another came and, after filling a bath with scalding water, thrust him in and were about to scrub him with a bar of some kind of grease when Hari leaped from the bath and, falling on his knees, begged them not to touch him with it.

"It is only soap," said one of those who had been sent to bathe him.

"Ah, good sir," replied Hari, "I mean no offense. But I have heard that what you call soap is made of the fat of pigs and if I am touched with it, then my immortal soul will be defiled and I can never gain the Paradise promised us by the prophet of the One God."

The bath attendants looked at each other in surprise, for it seemed that none of them knew what the soap was made of.

"Hell, we use it all the time," said one.

"Alas," said Hari, "that is one reason (though not the only one) why you Franks can never gain eternal bliss." But the men said that the soap was made only from vegetable fats and returned Hari to the bath, where they scrubbed him unmercifully, washing away the little charcoal mark on his forehead which averted

16

the Evil Eye and another on his cheek which announced that he was of the Tribe of the Lion. The rites of the first set of priests having robbed him of his physical privacy, those of this second set robbed him of his spiritual identity; and having then, as he felt, been reduced to nothing, he was left alone for a while wrapped in a huge towel.

"Perhaps all is as it should be," he said. "I have heard that in some religions it is held that a man must be so humbled as to become nothing at all before he can enter Heaven. And so I am to be robbed of my privacy of person and of my spiritual identity and of all guards against the evils of the world in order to be admitted to the Best of All Possible Nations. Indeed, even my blood is to be examined to see whether it is of sufficient purity and also my urine. Is it possible that theirs is of a different color? But since it is necessary to submit to these things, undoubtedly I will be recompensed by the glories and the happiness with which I will be surrounded on my arrival."

Hari was now faint with hunger and at last was permitted to eat breakfast; but while he did so, there being, it seemed, a great need for haste, he was questioned by a man who apparently had control over the admission of immigrants—even the guests of Presidents—into the Best of All Possible Nations. To some questions he was able to give a straightforward answer, as for instance whether he had at any time belonged to any party whose object it was to overthrow the government of the nation he was now preparing to visit.

"Not at all," said Hari, "and that for a very good

17

reason. Until those gentlemen appeared to me I had never even heard of your nation."

"It is impossible that you never heard of our nation," said the questioner. "Why, we have spent several billions of dollars in your country."

"Indeed?" said Hari. "I did not know that my country had so much for sale. What did you buy?"

"Buy?" said the man. "Nothing. We just gave the money away. For good will."

"That is something that cannot be bought but is to be obtained only by excellence of character," said Hari. "What a pity that you did not first talk to the Sadhu in my village who could have told you so, and all that money would have been saved."

"What is the name of this Sadhu?" asked the man.

"Punjat Tremor Raki," said Hari.

"Age?"

"He is said to be three hundred and fifty years old. He has a white beard of great beauty."

"And what has he to say about our foreign aid program?"

"Not one word," said Hari, "for he has not heard of it."

"What does he say about money then?"

"Very little. He has none."

"But he is against gifts of money. You told me so yourself."

"No. He says that a man can do no more good in the world than exists in himself and neither then can a people do more good than exists in themselves, for you cannot give what you have not got. Therefore he says that it is necessary for a man or a people to first per-

18

fect himself before he attempts to perfect others. Also the only gifts that can be made between people are gifts of love. In whatever form those gifts are made, whether of goods or of money or of help, if they are not gifts of love but only gifts intended for the profit of the giver then nothing has been given and nothing has been received."

"So if I gave you a million dollars for reasons other than affection, according to your Sadhu, I would have given you nothing?"

"That is true," said Hari. "For all gifts must be a sharing, in love and compassion, of the life of another, or they are nothing."

"I will make a note of the name of your Sadhu for I think he is a Communist," said the man. "It is a hell of a note when we send ships of grain and ships of money to this country and all our efforts are defeated by a Red nut in every little village in the nation. Has he ever been to Moscow?"

"No," said Hari.

"Probably never moved out of his village," said the man. "It's amazing how they can still infiltrate them."

"Sir," said Hari, "the Sadhu is a most holy man and has twice made the pilgrimage of the Ganges. That is to say he has proceeded to the mouth of the sacred river and then followed it to its source, keeping the river on his right hand, and then crossed over and returned again to the mouth, again keeping the river on his right hand and making a circuit after the example of the sun, which we call in our country *pradakshina*."

"And no doubt in the course of this journey he contacted other sadhus in each village he came to?"

19

"Certainly," said Hari. "They would welcome him with food and flowers."

So the man wrote "Communist Organizer" in his book after the name of the Sadhu Punjat Tremor Raki and then went on with his questioning.

Hari's race was settled as Caucasian, his religion as Muslim, his politics as possibly tinged with communism but certainly of the left, and in this latter he barely passed the standard of his examiner. Although it seemed a little early in the day to be discussing such matters, he now found himself closely pressed with questions about his sexual prowess and concluded that this was to see whether he could make a proper contribution to the happiness of the ladies in the Best of All Possible Nations.

Since he had been taught never to brag of any activity, he modestly admitted that he had delayed his first sexual adventure until his eleventh birthday when, coming upon the Sadhu's widowed daughter in need, he had done what he could to satisfy her wants. He had, he said, continued in this pleasant and charitable work with eagerness. Pressed for figures, he said he believed he had in the ten years since his first adventure introduced fifty virgins to the satisfactions of this activity, and consoled perhaps two hundred widows or wives whose husbands were either neglecting them or had gone on long journeys.

"In that case," said the examiner, who had seemed very interested during the questioning and had many times pressed for more detailed answers, "there can be no question of your being allowed to visit our nation."

"You mean I have failed?" cried Hari. "My performance is not judged up to the standards of the men of your nation?"

"On the contrary," said the examiner, "you are excluded on the grounds of moral turpitude."

"And what is that?" asked Hari.

"Sexual intercourse with others than your wife," was the reply.

"But I have no wife," said Hari.

"Then you should not indulge in sexual activities."

"Is this really the case with all the unmarried men and women of your country?" demanded Hari.

"As to that," said his examiner, "the answer is plainly no. But whatever the moral quality of our own citizens, we demand that to visit us all aliens be either married or virgins. While it is true that lechery of every kind abounds in our nation, that the books that sell most are those that contrive to give the most intimate and exciting accounts of sexual activity of every kind, and while magazines depicting men and women in lewd circumstances and postures are to be found in every drugstore, freely for sale, nonetheless we do not want our citizens corrupted by foreigners of loose morals. No, I am afraid I cannot allow you to enter our country. You must be barred permanently from obtaining a visa of any kind."

The examiner then said that he would contact President Pangloss and tell him that the first elephant boy picked to be his guest had to be excluded on grounds of moral turpitude. And such is the waywardness of the human heart that Hari, who up to this point had not really wanted to go to the Best of All Possible Nations, but would have preferred to return to his be-

21

loved Golden Lotus, now found that he was bitterly disappointed at being prohibited from ever visiting Dr. Pangloss' country.

He pleaded to be told if there was any way possible in which he could atone for his unconscious wrong-doing but was told that there was none.

He was then very despondent and went to see Bud and Sam, for whom he had begun to develop some affection, to make his adieus. Sam inquired why he was so sad and, having been told the reason, he and Hari went immediately to see the immigration officer once again.

"Listen," he said, "you've got this guy wrong. First of all you have to remember that he isn't a Christian. Now under his religion he is probably entitled to get all he can. No penalties. So if we exclude him on grounds of moral turpitude, which are grounds laid down in Christian ethics, we are interfering with his religious beliefs by forcing Christian principles on someone who is not a Christian. So if you want to avoid a big stink about this in the papers at home—not to mention the papers out here, if they have any—you'd better forget all about that moral turpitude stuff and give him his visa."

"There are, I suppose, possibilities of international repercussions," said the immigration officer.

"Right," said Sam. "In most parts of the world sexual intercourse is regarded as a matter of private rather than government concern. How the hell we ever got into the act I'll never know."

The matter was then ended satisfactorily and Hari

received permission to visit the Best of All Possible Nations as the guest of Dr. Pangloss.

The plane ride itself, across half the world, proved of great benefit to Hari in preparing him for his visit to Dr. Pangloss and his country.

Chapter Three

A MILITARY plane had been sent to bring Hari from India and because of the need for carrying extra fuel, all its guns had been taken off, the weight thus saved being used for gasoline storage. The pilot, Captain John Mitchell, had his name printed on the front of his flight suit; and before boarding the plane Sam and Bud pinned name labels on themselves and put one on Hari, and he assumed that this was done so that if any of them should become lost they could readily be identified by their labels.

The first several hours (they had taken off at dawn on the day following Hari's ordeals at the hands of his examiners) were spent flying over the tawny hide of India, the yellow of the ground being relieved here and there by streams which drew a tatter of green along their length. Near such rivers were hundreds of squares of rice paddies and, farther out, fields of millet. But there were few forests and only occasional clumps of mango trees or of palms of different kinds.

There were, however, like brightly colored scraps dropped on the ground, hundreds of villages, each with a little cultivated area around it, which drew from Sam the remark that India was a nation of villages.

"Surely this is true of every country," said Hari, and was surprised to learn that villages, though they still existed in Bud's country, were dying as people found it necessary to earn their living in manufacturing centers in small or big cities.

"They have better housing, earn more money, have better sanitation facilities, hot and cold water, electricity, better transportation, hospitals, doctors, libraries and movie houses," said Sam.

"But this has surely destroyed all your communities," said Hari. "Or do communities of friends and neighbors and families all move together into the city so that they can continue to enjoy each other's company?"

"Who needs neighbors and friends?" asked Sam. "We got television."

But Bud was interested in village life and Hari eager to talk about it. He explained that it was hard to believe that anywhere else in the world there was so much variety in living as in a village. Each season was looked forward to with enthusiasm and remembered with affection. Each birth affected all and each death also. Kinship was both intricate and strong and the fortune of one brought rejoicing to many and no man ever sorrowed alone. None were much hungrier than others or fuller than others; and though there were spites and quarrels, nonetheless these only added interest to village life and no serious harm ever resulted from them.

Marriages called for community celebrations which lasted not for an hour or two but for a week. Big feasts were given and splendid dances performed, the dancers making their own costumes. Bells were rung and cymbals clashed and zithers played and horns blown. The water buffalo rejoiced in their own cumbersome way, cleaning their nostrils with enormous tongues, and so did the ticbirds on their backs, pecking off the lice on which they thrived. If something new was brought into the village, it was a source of pleasure for everybody, not merely the owner; the prayer flags mounted on bamboo poles at the entrance to the village like so many pennons on the heads of lances made prayers both gay and public, so that all knew the desires of each person and how these desires were treated when, the prayer flag having disintegrated in the wind, the prayer was received in Heaven.

"When I die," said Hari, "I will be mourned by the whole village, which will be at least three hundred people. They will follow me to the burial ground and I will be buried in such a position as to be able to leap out of my grave at the first sounding of the trumpet. Also, in the meantime, various devices will be put about my grave to keep off devils."

Bud reflected soberly that when he died the only result would be the enrichment of an undertaker. Many of his friends would not even know of his death and those who did would soon forget about it. He felt sad.

"I'll take television," said Sam.

The plane, having thundered over India, now rent the skies of Burma, the land changing from lion yellow to moss green and then an even deeper hue of green, the huge trees of the forests, their exteriors swathed in vines, straining upwards to the life-giving sun. Clouds the size of continents moved imperiously about the heavens and Hari, having consulted both the sun and the plane's compass, prostrated himself on the floor to say his prayers.

It became evident in a little while that the plane had changed direction and Captain Mitchell, having put the controls on automatic pilot and passed out some sandwiches, informed his passengers that they were heading south to avoid both some rough air and hostile country below.

"We will have to fly over a small part of Sasia, where we are at war with the Baddies, but there is nothing to worry about," he said. "You are traveling in the best of all possible military airplanes. The pilot model cost ten billion dollars and the careers of two senators to produce. This plane can fly faster than any pursuer, higher than any antiaircraft missile, take off in slightly less than its own length, do Immelmanns, rolls and barrel turns in the space of its own wingspan. It is powered by twin turbojets developing one hundred thousand horsepower each, and the air frame is of monocoque tubular aluminum made by a company owned by one of the senators to whom I have just referred.

"The fuselage is both heliarced and riveted to the frame; and transverse, prestressed, circular-sectioned bulkheads are added every four feet as additional reinforcement. When she's carrying guns her armament is the equivalent of a heavy cruiser of the Second World War, and her rate of fire is that of fifteen divisions of the Napoleonic Army which butchered the whole of Spain. The accuracy of the gun-pointing mechanism is such that in tests over the Mohave Desert a single burst, the equivalent of three broadsides simultaneously fired from the battle cruiser *California*, took a single tail feather out of a desert hawk without causing any other injury to the bird, which, however, died of convulsions.

"The plane is at present flying on a programmed tape with instructions to take the Glinjit Pass through the eastern mountains of Sasia, and the programming is so accurate that the plane will make all necessary rudder and elevation adjustments to fly accurately down this pass. The peanut butter sandwiches are supplied courtesy of the Nine Thousandth and Eighty-sixth Fighter Reconnaissance Light Bomber Peace Control Command and the coffee is supplied courtesy of your nearest USO."

While they were eating their sandwiches a wing fell off the plane; and, aided by its two one-hundred-thousand-horsepower jets, it plunged earthward to bury itself in the bowels of a rice paddy a distance of three hundred yards, or the equivalent of ten of its kind, placed end to end.

Chapter Four

WHEN Hari recovered consciousness he found himself lying on his back in a dark gray ooze in which he could feel that he was slowly sinking. His head ached as if it had been split by an ax and he had the distinct feeling that his feet had been taken from him and given to someone else.

This feeling was aroused by the fact that he could feel a pull on them and also a pressure on them which he knew (befuddled though he was) was not being exerted by himself. It was some time before his brain, throbbing in great waves of pain followed by short troughs of relief, sorted out this sensation to produce the conclusion that he was being dragged through the ooze by his legs. The sensation of sinking resulted from quantities of ooze piling up around him.

He concluded that he was being taken either to Heaven or to Hell by an angel of the Prophet and, considering the method used, had a suspicion that it was to the latter place that he was going. But there

29

seemed nothing he could do about it and, the rage of his head being now reinforced by a clashing of cymbals of enormous size, he subsided with relief into an unconscious state, his last sensation being one of gratitude that it was possible to avoid the torments of Hell by fainting.

When he once more recovered his senses he knew that he had been sent to the infernal regions where darkness, fire, thirst, and ugliness are combined in an amalgam of terror. He opened his eyes to be aware of a huge orange flame burning on his left and, leaning over him, a female Djinn or devil so ugly that, had he had the power, he would have screamed.

This monstress had lost the tip of her nose, and the bone of the skull seemed to show through the two terrible holes that led into her head for breathing purposes. She had also entirely lost one eye. The eye was not merely blind. It was gone, leaving a sunken area of horror to the left of her nose. The other eye, the right eye, was still present, but glittered with ferocity through squinting lids.

On its head this Djinn had the hair of the damned—that is to say, hair composed of the black intestines of serpents—and she had two teeth, one in the upper and one in the lower jaw, but, alas, they did not meet.

"Allah have mercy," said Hari, and closed his eyes, and the prayer brought a screech from the woman, who cried, "He is alive."

Comforted by the sound of a human voice (though only in the smallest degree), Hari opened his eyes again to find an old man, quite bald, and with large portions of his facial tissue gone, peering down on him together with the hag.

"Who are you?" he cried.

"I am a farmer and this is my wife," said the man.

"Allah be praised," said Hari. "I thought I was in Hell."

"Why, so you are," said the man, "for this is Sasia, where a war for liberty, so we are told, has been raging for thirty years or more. You must certainly have led an evil life that of all places in the world for your airplane to have tumbled from the sky it tumbled here. Are you one of the Baddies?"

"No."

"Are you one of the Goodies?"

"I do not know."

"Then you are one of the Unfortunates like us, that is to say neither of the Good Party nor of the Bad Party, and thus a mere unimportant victim," said the man; and the woman picked Hari up in her sticklike arms, held him to her withered bosom and crooned over him like a mother over a child. Hari was astounded at this reaction and, when the woman finally released him, surprised to find tears streaming from her good eye and also from the socket from which the other eyeball was absent, so that she wept with both her light and her darkness.

"He is like our son, Pinji," said the woman; and with hands which were withered to claws, she reached out to stroke Hari's hair, which was entirely anointed with ooze.

"All young men are like our son Pinji," said her

31

husband. "In this it might be said that Pinji never dies."

"Then when he was burned to death all young men were at that moment burned to death," said the woman.

"We must be thankful for small mercies," said her husband. "He was immolated with napalm. It might have been gasoline, which is uncivilized. In any case this one needs help. Let us do what we can for him."

Hari had by now concluded that, having survived by a miracle, he had fallen into the hands of madmen. Never having been schooled in psychiatry or psychology (or indeed in any kind of witchcraft), he knew that the insane are to be treated with a special care and consideration, being under the protection of Allah. He therefore begged the man and his wife not to be concerned about him, but to take their ease and rest after the labor of dragging him to wherever he was, and he would in a little while recover and then be able to do something in return to help them.

"What is your name, sir?" asked the man.

"I am Hari Ranjit Singh," he replied, and decided to say nothing further for the present.

"And I am Didji Moda, which in my language means Son of the Mountain and this is my wife, Celestial Flower." Celestial Flower now wiped the tears from her good eye and from her eye socket and, having brought the bottom of a rusty can in which there was a little water, commenced to clean Hari, who was somewhat embarrassed, being at the time completely naked.

"I hope you will pardon us," said Son of the Moun-

32

tain. "When we found you in the field after your airplane had crashed, we took your clothing for we have nothing here at all but a few rags, and cloth of any kind, then, is very valuable to us. But I will bring every article to you and you will find nothing missing."

"If you thought me dead why did you drag me here?" asked Hari.

"To see if you had any gold teeth," said Celestial Flower. "If you had, we would have knocked them out and been able to sell them to a person we know for a little food. But although we must go hungry as a result, I am truly glad that you are alive. For you are a young man as was our son Pinji and we are old and must soon die anyway."

"Are things indeed so wretched with you that you must rob corpses?" asked Hari indignantly.

"It is a curious thing," said Son of the Mountain, "that those who make corpses are heroes and those who merely rob them are villains. But we will discuss this and other matters when we have eaten a little of this nourishing rat soup, to which my good wife was able to add the intestines of a small lizard she caught only this morning," and he gazed on his wife with the affection of a man for one who has produced a dish of the greatest excellence.

Hari, between his miraculous escape from death, his bursting headache, the clashing of the cymbals in his ears (for these symptoms still continued, though a little abated) and the stench of the mud from the paddy (for the pitiful amount of water brought him by Celestial Flower had served only to spread the mud over him more evenly), had no appetite for a broth of rat and lizard intestines. But the politeness of his village upbringing demanded that he taste the brew.

Taste it he did then, and found it not unpleasant. He swallowed a spoonful or two and then excused himself from taking more, saying that he had just devoured a hearty meal before the wing fell off the airplane which had cost so much money and wrecked the careers of two senators. Son of the Mountain and Celestial Flower, therefore, with considerable nicety finished the remainder of the soup between them, and picked on the delicate little bones of the rats. Celestial Flower, having only two teeth which did not meet, could but suck on the bones and then give them to Son of the Mountain, who having in the back of his mouth some molars in opposition to one another was able to grind them up and swallow them down.

While this meal was in progress, Hari examined his surroundings and found that he was in a cave and the orange light which he had taken to be the flames of Hell was actually a crude torch made by stuffing a rough wick of dried grasses into the neck of a bottle containing oil.

"We are not the first to live in this cave," said Son of the Mountain, "for in the back there is a small passage and beyond this a larger cave. And in this cave there are skulls which are like ours in many respects and yet different. I think they are the skulls of men who lived here many hundreds of thousands of years ago."

"Some of these skulls," said Celestial Flower, "have openings in the sides or in the bottom. It is plain that these openings were made so that others might scoop out and eat the brains."

"They were then cannibals?" cried Hari in horror. "How can you stay in such a place?"

"Sir," said Son of the Mountain, "if you had seen what we have seen, you would run to the arms of cannibals for protection and for comfort. If it will amuse you I will tell you something of our story. It will perhaps help you to forget the hurts that still trouble you."

"I would be very glad to hear it, indeed," said Hari.

So Celestial Flower heaped some damp turfs of grass and earth around the fire to make it last the longer, and Son of the Mountain commenced his tale.

Chapter Five

"You must know," said Son of the Mountain, "that a war has been raging in this country for the past thirty years and, no end being in sight, is likely to continue for thirty years more or perhaps for a hundred years more. Indeed, how it can be ended nobody can tell because, to tell you the truth, nobody knows what was the beginning of it. It is entirely possible that this war which has a hundred causes or no cause at all, according to your point of view, may become perpetual or bring in the whole of the eastern portions of the world and eventually the whole world itself.

"Whether this happens and if it does happen whether people will then know what the war is about, is beyond my ability to tell you."

"I do not wish to be impolite," said Hari, "but surely you are exaggerating or expressing a partisan point of view because of your apparent sufferings from the war."

"Not at all," said Son of the Mountain. "If you will listen to me patiently, then you will yourself understand how this state of affairs has come into being.

"In the beginning, that is to say about thirty years ago, this country was invaded by the Baddies, whose own lands lying not far away across a stretch of sea, were becoming overpopulated. War is a great corrector of population problems, the other corrector—that is, moderation in sexual intercourse—being far too painful to apply. The Baddies, in any case, having overpopulated their lands, decided to invade these, where they would on the one hand have more room, and on the other hand kill off sufficient of themselves and of our people to provide even further room.

"If another excuse for the war was needed, then there was the necessity for the Baddies to exercise their army, which they had allowed to grow to enormous proportions both to solve the unemployment problem in their country (brought about by overpopulation) and in preparation for the invasion of our nation.

"It is forgotten now whether the Baddies announced that our nation had insulted theirs beyond all pardon or disposed with that formality. They launched their armies on the land, and these armies, being victorious, set about enjoying the fruits of victory, which is to say that they looted, burned, tortured, shot, butchered, beheaded, imprisoned, destroyed, raped, and did whatever else they wished. Those of us who survived this looked forward eagerly to the day when they would be overcome and we would be able to return to our work, which was mostly farming or fishing."

"Then it would be correct to say that the original

37

cause of the war was the invasion of your country by the army of the Baddies," said Hari.

"Not at all," said his host. "For at that time we had already been invaded and our country taken over by the Goodies."

"The Goodies?" cried Hari.

"They come from the West," said Son of the Mountain. "You may take it as a general rule that the Goodies are from the West and the Baddies are from the East. That is to say in international affairs. In the internal affairs of nations the geographical axis is not east and west but north and south—as, for instance, in America the Northern states against the Southern states, also in Ireland, Northern Ireland versus Southern Ireland, and also in Korea, Northern Korea against Southern Korea, and now my own country is engaged in a national-international war which also pits the North against the South."

"National-international. I do not know what that means for it is surely a contradiction."

"When two countries wish to test their strength, their army efficiency, and their new bombs and in general exercise their military parts they quite often find another country to fight in so that they themselves are not damaged in their homelands," said Son of the Mountain. "This leads to a national-international civil war such as took place some years ago in Spain, and many times in Poland and also in the smaller countries of Europe and now in our country.

"However, to return to the war which has now been raging here for thirty years, it cannot be said that the Baddies were the first instigators, as I pointed out the

38

Goodies had invaded us beforehand. They said that their object was to protect their citizens, a few of whom had been allowed to settle here and trade.

"Be that as it may, our masters, the Goodies, were defeated by the Baddies. We now were caught between the upper and lower grindstones of two war machines. If we did not help and cooperate with the Baddies, we were imprisoned, starved, flogged, burned, or skewered by bayonets according to the degree of our non-co-operation. On the other hand, if to avoid such a fate befalling ourselves or our wives and children, we did cooperate with the Baddies, we were promised by the Goodies that we would be imprisoned, starved, flogged, burned or beheaded (they have a different custom in the matter of death) according to the degree of our co-operation.

"We were of course compelled to supply a great number of our women for the pleasure of the Goodies in their day and then a great number for the pleasure of the Baddies in their day. Indeed, it became the mark of the women of my country, whatever their age, that seeing a soldier, they would immediately lie down, close their eyes, and endure whatever was done; and this leads me to a point which I have often pondered, and that is the self-defeating nature of the task of the soldier."

"I have never heard mention of this," said Hari. "Please enlighten me."

"The self-defeating nature of the soldier lies in this," said the other. "With one weapon the soldier destroys life and with the other he creates it, and he uses both

39

weapons without discrimination and with equal vigor and enthusiasm.

"But to return to my tale. After seven years of warfare in our country between the Goodies and the Baddies, the Baddies were finally defeated and the Goodies decided to once more reassert their mastery over us.

"At this point, however, the novel thought occurred to some of our people that there was little to choose between one and the other, and the Baddies having gone, the Goodies could be sent packing after them.

"So a revolt was staged and the garrisons of the Goodies attacked, and in this our people were encouraged by the people of the Best of All Possible Nations, who said that it was certainly wrong that any nation should live subject to another and who assured us that their own nation had itself once been subject to the rule of others, but the people had risen, thrown off their bonds, and asserted their independence—curiously with the assistance of those same Goodies who were now our oppressors.

"Be that as it may, we revolted and defeated the Goodies and were preparing to hold an election to establish a government after the manner of that of the Best of All Possible Nations when disaster descended on us again."

"How did this happen?" asked Hari.

"It is unfortunate concerning elections that they are contests and there are those who will win and those who will lose. Also it is not sufficient in an election to merely elect. It is important that those elected meet with the approval of others more powerful. Thus, as the time for our election came closer, it appeared to the nobles and royalty who in the past had been accustomed to rule us, and indeed who had held favored positions under both the Goodies and the Baddies, that their party would lose the election and they would be thrown out, lose their fortune and positions, and the country be ruled instead by a body of people who were neither of the royalty nor of the nobility.

"These then, claiming to be our government though never elected to that position, announced that no election could be held. Our nation was immediately divided and both sides armed themselves, for what cannot be decided by ballot these days will certainly be decided by bullet.

"So the war of the Goodies against the Baddies, which was followed by our revolt against the Goodies, now became a civil war in which the party supporting the nobles were the Goodies and those opposing them were the Baddies."

"One moment," said Hari. "All this talk of Goodies and Baddies is confusing me. Is it not true that those whom you now call Baddies are really Communists and those whom you call Goodies are Capitalists?"

"That is entirely possible and it is also beside the point," said the other. "In the early days of this war, when I was a comparatively young man, I was told that this was so and that if the Communists were to succeed they would take away my farm and make me work for nothing. But my father, who was then alive, pointed out that this would be nothing new. For under the previous system, though we retained our farm, we were taxed so heavily that the profits went to the governments. It is a choice for philosophers—whether a

41

man is happier hungry under communism or hungry under capitalism.

"The point is that whether we have a Communist government or a Capitalist government is of no importance to us who are peasants and rice farmers. We would rather have a Communist peace than a Capitalist war, or, lest I be accused of partiality, a Capitalist peace than a Communist war. The whole argument about communism and capitalism is indulged in by people who are not exposed to suffering and death on either side, but direct policies and armies from the safety of beautiful buildings.

"It is these who coin the rousing phrases; who denounce those who do not support them as cowards and traitors to their country; who hustle the young men into their graves and believe that in so doing, they are creating heroes.

"How heroic it is indeed to denounce communism in a Capitalist country! And how patriotic and worthy to denounce capitalism in a Communist country! But I have looked on dead men from both sides and been struck by an appalling similarity between them."

"Such as what?" asked Hari.

"They are dead; they are young; and they could not be trusted to vote," said Son of the Mountain.

"But to continue with my tale of this impossible war. When it became evident to the Southern Democracy of Royalty that matters were going badly, they thought to get help from the Best of All Possible Nations. And this nation generously sent officers to advise on military strategy and tactics. In a little while, however, the war going even more heavily against the

Southern section, more men and more officers arrived from that peace-loving nation until there are now more of the scoundrels in this country than there are of our own soldiers.

"These have now told us, 'We are not here to wage war. We are here to wage peace.' For this we must all be truly grateful. For in the interests of waging peace they have poured fire over our lands, burned women and children by the score, oblitered villages, removed thousands of families from their homes, destroyed our farms, turned farmers into refugees and refugees into criminals, consoled themselves with our women and consoled their consciences by taking care of a few of the orphans whose parents they have butchered. So if this is what results from the waging of peace on us, it is a blessing indeed that this Best of All Possible Nations has not decided to wage war on us.

"So you see now how it is that I say nobody knows what this war is about. We were better off in the days of the Goodies and the Baddies. To be sure, both insisted that they were here for our benefit, but they did not insist upon being believed and although that is a small point it is also an important one. It is hard indeed to have all your children killed, your wife turned into a prostitute, yourself made to suffer this, your lands despoiled and your home torn down and then be told that this is all for your own good—and be called a traitor to freedom if you do not proclaim in a loud voice that you believe this is so.

"I have questioned my wife closely on the matter of being violated and she has assured me that she does not feel spiritually elevated after being raped by a

Goodie, nor especially soiled after being raped by a Baddie, and in this matter there is nothing to choose between Capitalist and Communist. So also in the matter of the destruction of my sons, of whom I had five. Three were killed by Communists and two by Capitalists. But though you may accuse me of a lack of nicety of feeling it makes no difference to me whether they died in one cause or another. I only know that they are dead and I will never see them again and do not dare to think of them."

"Have you any daughters, sir?" asked Hari.

"Yes, indeed," said Son of the Mountain. "We have a daughter, Moon Lily, and we have managed to save her. She was a baby when this war broke out and, thinking of her safety, we put her in a convent. But after the convent had been twice overrun by soldiers of both sides we could see that there was no safety for her there. Nor was there safety here at home, for my wife lost her eye fighting for Moon Lily, and I was myself castrated for trying to protect her.

"After these private misfortunes, which can hardly be hoped to have advanced the cause of either capitalism or communism, I decided that prostitution might provide for Moon Lily the protection which Christianity could not. Therefore I sent her at the age of twelve to a big city where there are many of the soldiers of our allies and I hear that she has a place to put her sleeping mat on the pavement outside the railroad station and by serving a dozen or more customers a night, is able to earn enough to live."

"A dozen a night?" cried Hari. "Surely the price is higher than that?"

"Not at all," said Son of the Mountain. "For when young men have been forced to leave their own country to fight for your liberty (as they are told) then they feel that in exchange for risking their lives, they are certainly entitled to free sexual intercourse with the citizens. So many give her nothing at all. Some beat her. But then, some pay. And she says she has never encountered one of the clergy of our allies who did not pay promptly and so it is plain that after all there is something to be said for religion."

There came now, from the mouth of the cave, the sound of footsteps and of men grunting and cursing. Celestial Flower immediately threw a pan of muddy water over the fire but she was too late. Several soldiers rushed into the cave and dragged the three of them out into the moonlight, where they were examined by the soldiers, who established that Son of the Mountain was a man, Celestial Flower was a woman and Hari was a stranger.

They, therefore, following the usages of war in civilized nations, shot Son of the Mountain, raped Celestial Flower and took Hari into custody for questioning.

Chapter Six

HARI was soon taken to the camp of his captors, who turned out to be Baddies of the Second Time Around. There he was brought before a colonel who demanded to know all about him. Hari had no difficulty answering the questions put to him but the greatest difficulty getting anyone to believe his answers.

Whenever he got to that portion of his story in which he confessed that he, an elephant boy, was going to the Best of All Possible Nations at the invitation of the President, Dr. Pangloss, he was taken outside and bastinadoed, or beaten on the soles of his feet with a bamboo cane until he had fainted. This happened four times before he decided that, the truth being punishable, a lie might be rewarded. He therefore changed his story and said that he was a steward employed on the plane which had lost a wing; that he had survived the crash only to be dragged to the cave to be robbed by Son of the Mountain and his wife, and had now fallen into the hands of the Baddies, whom, he said, despite his feet which were now swollen to the size of puddings, he regarded as saviors and brothers.

"That is better," said the colonel. "You surely do not expect us to believe that a mere elephant boy was to be received by Dr. Pangloss, when our own leader, after twenty years of warfare, has been unable to get a single word directly from him. But are you truly a friend and brother to liberty?"

"I am indeed," said Hari fervently.

"And do you regard nothing as so horrible as being enslaved and exploited by the capitalist oppressors?"

"These have been my sentiments since I first heard of the situation," said Hari.

"Then I am pleased to receive you as a volunteer into the People's Liberation Army," said the colonel. "You will be prepared to march in an hour."

Having, as a volunteer, the choice of marching or being once again beaten on the feet with a bamboo cane, Hari decided with enthusiasm that he would march and was soon introduced to his comrades in the People's Liberation Army, who were many of them enthusiastic volunteers like himself. An officer gave him a bowl of rice, a gun and a number; and a little while later a medal was pinned on his chest by the same colonel who had inducted him into the army.

"What is that for?" asked Hari.

"For volunteering to give all your pay to the cause of freedom," said the colonel, pinning the medal on him. "Kindly put your foot on the ground. You are dripping blood on my boots." It appeared that the whole regiment had volunteered to give their pay in the same way, and the colonel spoke to them movingly of the heroic solidarity they were showing in the struggle to free their brothers from the accursed Imperialist and Capitalist tyrants.

"And now, brothers and comrades," said the colonel, "the great opportunity of striking a blow for the freedom of the proletariat for which you have been training arduously is at hand. This very night we are to be given the chance to join the immortals of our militant revolution in flinging ourselves bodily at the very heartland of the enemy. The eyes of the workers of the world will be upon you and although, if you are killed, you will only become so much manure (for the concept of a life after death is a Capitalist lie intended to make the slave content with his chains), still you will have the satisfaction of knowing that you are Communist manure, which is the very best sort.

"Let us go forward then, comrades, and either achieve victory or enrich the soil with our bodies. Be sure, as you fling yourself into the maw of heroic slaughter, that I, your colonel, will be close behind you, plotting even greater victories for the future."

From this Hari concluded that the regiment was to attack some formidable stronghold of the enemy.

"What is the name of this place?" he asked one of his comrades, for he was sure that he was going to be killed if, indeed, he did not die on the march to the attack and such is the peculiarity of human nature that knowing the name of the place at which he would meet his end would give him some slight comfort.

"Wadjak," said the other.

"And is it indeed a very strongly fortified place?"

"Nothing of the sort," said the soldier. "It is a small

village with no defenses in which live only a few old men, some women and their children."

"Then why should we destroy it?" asked Hari, though he was very relieved to know what the formidable enemy force was that was to be engaged and began to hope that if he survived the march, he might also survive the fighting.

"For a very good and sufficient reason," said the soldier. "The colonel owes a hundred thousand piasters to the headman of the village, who is foolish enough to refuse to cancel the debt. So the colonel is about to give him payment. Indeed, the inhuman insistence of the money-lending Capitalists that debts be paid has driven many into the People's Liberation Army. Though others of us, as you are aware, volunteered for other reasons."

"And are there really none among you who truly believe that in fighting you are liberating the people?" asked Hari, who wanted to keep talking so as to forget the pain of his feet.

"The political ambitions of the people of this country do not extend beyond a bowl of rice and a safe place to raise their children," replied the soldier. "Unfortunately all our leaders, including a greater number of our officers, are mad."

"In what way mad?" asked Hari.

"They think otherwise," said the soldier. "They think we are concerned about whether we are Communists or whether we are Capitalists, and if Communists whether we are reformist, deviationist, syndicalist, radical, Marxist, Chinese, Albanian, confessing, secret, economic or cultural, or economic-cultural-

49

revisionist. And if Capitalists whether imperialist, monopolist, liberal, conservative, republican, autocratic, oligarchic, progressive, retrogressive, unionist, royalist, conservative-republican with oligarchic sympathies or any combination of these. In plain truth we are interested only in staying alive, and it is to stay alive and not advance the cause of capitalism or communism in any of their variations that I and most of my comrades joined this army."

"How can that be so?" asked Hari. "Surely the life of a soldier is extremely dangerous."

"On the contrary," said the other. "In wartime it is the life of the civilian which is dangerous and the soldier lives in comparative security. For one thing he is frequently fed, so he will not die of starvation, is clothed and often housed, so he will not die of exposure, receives medical attention and is exempt from being shot out of hand, hanged, burned, tortured and so on. That of course is because in time of war a soldier is valuable. Nothing, you understand, has less use during hostilities than a dead soldier.

"On the other hand nobody looks after the civilian in time of war, and being without protection, he is preyed upon by the soldiers of any army that happens to pass his way. He can starve. He can die of exposure. He can die of wounds. He can be put to death on suspicion. He and his village can be attacked and destroyed on the suspicion of sympathizing with the enemy. The civilian may be arrested for espionage by one side or the other and beaten or shot without trial. His food may be seized, his farm ruined, his animals killed. I assure you, my friend, that in time of war only a fool or a man of exceptional courage remains a civil-ian. Myself, being a coward, joined this army. In this war, the number of civilians who have died far exceed the number of soldiers on either side. Were you not yourself, as a civilian, caned on the feet? But now as a soldier you are quite safe except in case of a battle, when you still have a chance of perhaps as much as ten to one of escaping without hurt."

This view of the safety of the soldier as opposed to that of the civilian in time of war was so novel that Hari was for some time lost in thinking it over, and even forgot his feet, which, since they were walking through flooded rice fields (or such he took them to be), were soon so chilled that he could scarcely feel any hurt in them.

The sky was overcast, and although there was a full moon, not a ray of its light was able to penetrate the murk overhead. The regiment therefore marched in some disorder as it was extremely hard for one man to keep in touch with his comrades ahead of him. Finally they crossed over the flooded area of the rice fields and then were required to wade over a river. Hari, because of his injured feet, fell down in midstream and his comrade soldiers, glad to find so firm a footing placed at their disposal, walked over him. Indeed he would have drowned had he not spent the greater part of his child-hood in a river playing with Golden Lotus, who some-times undertook to hold him playfully under the water with her trunk. He had then great ability in the mat-ter of holding his breath, and when the last man had used him as a foothold he surfaced and struggled after them. He was, then, several minutes late in regaining his comrades on the other bank and the officer told him that he was, as a result, to be fined two hundred piasters for lack of zeal in marching to hurl himself at the enemy.

On the other side of the river there were a number of trees, fairly evenly spaced one from the other and with no underbrush about so that it was clear that they were in a plantation.

The officer took out a pocket compass, glanced at it and called Hari. "The village is in that direction," he said. "It is probable, however, that the villagers have pickets posted. Go forward and discover if this is so and report back in ten minutes."

"But I have no experience as a scout," Hari protested.

"You have already been fined for lack of zeal," said the officer. "Take care lest some worse punishment is meted out to you. And walk carefully lest you betray your comrades, who now put all their trust in you."

Hari still pleaded that someone else be sent with him and with some reluctance the officer told another soldier to accompany Hari. Off they went then, Hari ahead and the other behind; and when they had gone only a few yards, the soldier raised his rifle to his shoulder, pointed it at Hari and said, "Now, comrade, on you go and find out about the pickets. Meanwhile I will stand here and cover you as a good comrade should."

Too late Hari realized that it had been indeed a mistake to ask for company on his errand, for now he was in danger not only from the enemy but from his own people. Nor had he the wit to go only a little farther and then, invisible in the dark, stay where he was for a short while and return with a report that he had come across no pickets.

He was not a seasoned campaigner, by any means, and so in ignorance of how things are done, he set about carrying out his order. His feet pained him so badly (some circulation being now restored since he was no longer wading through icy water) that he put them down with the greatest care on the ground and thus was able to move through the watching trees and darkness of the plantation in utmost silence.

He came upon no pickets and was surprised that not even a dog raised a sharp yap at him; for he knew that in his own country, the villages were guarded by flocks of vicious dogs. In fact, he was so successful in his scouting that he was able to enter the village and creep past several of the huts, in none of which was a light though he could hear sounds of snoring here and there. He saw, however, some chinks of light coming from a house towards the center of the village and, creeping to it, found a chink in the wall through which he could peer inside. There he saw the colonel of his regiment sitting at the table with another man who must surely be the headman or mayor of the village. They had a bottle of rice wine between them, and on the floor by the colonel's feet were several bulging bags which certainly contained money.

Hari immediately grasped the significance of this scene. The headman had forgiven the colonel's debt and even decided to lend him some more money. The attack therefore was not to take place and Hari, rejoicing, knew that if he was to save the lives of all the innocents in the village he must hurry back immediately and inform the officer of this change of plan.

Back he went as fast as he could stumble. He entirely forgot about his comrade, who, hearing him blundering through the brush, shot him through the leg. But with so many lives dependent on him, Hari still succeeded in dragging himself back to the regiment, though not in time. Before he could be brought to the officer a whistle was blown, there was a cumulative and fearful yell from all the men and they plunged through the plantation and descended on the village with grenades, machine guns, flamethrowers, and bayonets. Such was their fury that in moments the whole place was in flames, and those who did not escape the inferno were cut down by machine guns as they fled from the fire. Not a soul survived except the colonel.

He presented himself at the end of the action to congratulate his men on their solidarity and zeal for the people's revolution. But before he could say a word Hari cried out, "Alas, Colonel. What a disaster! All these innocent people killed! I did my best to get back here to say that all was well, that you were in the village with the headman who had forgiven you your debt and lent you more money, but I was too late."

"Take that pig," said the colonel, turning slowly on Hari, "and hang him up by his thumbs until he knows not to invent Capitalist lies to be spread about among his comrades with a view to destroying the confidence of the regiment in their comrade colonel."

One of the soldiers to carry out this task was the

same who had instructed Hari on the safety of the military life before the attack.

"You will never make a soldier, my friend," he said, tying Hari's thumbs together with a piece of rawhide, preparatory to hanging him by them from the branch of a tree. "You have not yet learned a soldier's first and most essential lesson."

"And what is that?" asked Hari.

"To keep your mouth shut," said the soldier, and with his comrades he hoisted Hari upward.

Chapter
Seven

Iт was fortunate for Hari that he was thus, for the second time, aloft though in such uncomfortable circumstances. To be sure, the pain of being suspended by his thumbs was such that he immediately fainted but the torture saved his life. He was hardly airborne before the Baddies were attacked by the Goodies with such energy that none escaped except the colonel, who had prudently retired to the rear with one or two trusted men to secure the money he had received from the village headman. The engagement was so fierce that the explosion of hand grenades, the racketing of guns and the lurid light and heat of the flamethrowers lasted for only a few minutes, when peace was restored accompanied by the smell of burning vegetation and flesh.

It was while they were counting the dead so as not to mislead the Press (a most important duty of soldiers) that Hari was discovered suspended from the tree.

"Poor son of a bitch," said the soldier who found him. "Just look what this poor bastard has endured for liberty."

He was about to cut Hari down when he remembered his responsibility to the public at home. He therefore called a combat correspondent who took several pictures (during which time Hari recovered consciousness and fainted again) and he was at last lowered to the ground and revived.

"Who are you?" he was asked.

"I am an elephant boy from India and the guest of Dr. Pangloss, President of the Best of All Possible Nations," he answered. Such a strange reply convinced his rescuers that Hari's sufferings had deprived him of his senses. And indeed it was very hard for Hari himself to believe that but three days before he had been in India, bathing in the Ganges with Golden Lotus and pouring a little warm water over her right eye, which was something she adored.

Hari therefore was evacuated by air to the capital of the Goodies' part of the country. There every attention was given him, and he soon recovered from his physical hurts, such was the excellence of the care he received. But his physical recuperation did not by any means put an end to his troubles, for since he constantly replied, when asked, that he was an elephant boy on his way to visit Dr. Pangloss, it was assumed that he was insane.

Psychiatrists were then called in to interview him and probe into his conscious and his subconscious, his infra-subconscious and his ultra-subconscious, his id and his ego, his subliminal horizons and the psycho-neuroticism which, it seemed, glowed around his thalamic regions.

It appeared that in the opinion of the psychiatrists something had gone wrong inside Hari's head about an inch and a half behind his left ear. Apparently this something was the result of a wish, suppressed from childhood, that his mother would drop dead. It was of no use for Hari to insist that his mother had died at his birth and he had no memory of her at all. It was explained to him that he merely thought that he had no memory of her. Nonetheless dark memories lingered in his mind of his mother even from the time that he was in her womb, that he resented the diet of highly spiced food which she ate and which gave him prenatal heartburn, and that when at his birth she had died, he had felt a sense of guilt that would last for the rest of his life, being convinced that he had killed her.

"But I did not kill my mother," cried Hari when this was all explained to him by Dr. Slicker, the chief psychiatrist.

"There will be no rest for you until you admit to yourself that you did," replied the psychiatrist, washing his hands—something which he performed every few minutes for he never seemed to get them clean to his own satisfaction.

"Now as to this Golden Lotus, an elephant to whom you are always referring and whom you keep pleading to be reunited with, she is merely a mother substitute. Having rejected your own mother, in point of fact killed her, you hope to ease the guilt and your own sense of loss by finding a substitute for her. Now it is very interesting that you did not find a human substitute but an animal substitute. This implies that your trauma may be much deeper than the results of the superficial examination I have been able to conduct so far would indicate. It suggests that in killing your mother, you were in fact attempting to kill off the whole human race."

"But I wasn't even three weeks old at the time," Hari protested.

Dr. Slicker ignored this. "Now the significance of an attempt to kill off the whole human race—turn your back on your species and join the nonhominids—lies in this," he said. "You are attempting to reverse the evolutionary process and flee from the present into the Ordovician or maybe even the Cambrian Era. That such a thing is possible is confirmed by both biologists and zoologists who have observed that creatures who a very short time ago lived in the splash zone beside the oceans of the world are now migrating into the water and taking up their life there totally submerged. Also man himself is deserting the land and attempting to live under the sea in specially constructed houses. And it is a fact known to every child that the whale once lived on dry land, also the seal and the porpoise, while the automobile—I mean the horse— once took its pleasure in the ocean.

"Now in your case, the important thing is to get over your feeling of guilt about killing your mother and wishing to slaughter the whole human race. I assure you that these feelings are entirely natural. Just about everybody would like to kill his mother and wipe out the whole neighborhood. Such feelings are what make us human."

After some time, it became apparent to Hari that he would never be released from the hospital and be rid of Dr. Slicker, who would continue to beat upon his mind without mercy, unless he adopted the same tactics he had with the colonel of the Baddies who up to that point had been beating on his feet. He therefore one day confessed to Dr. Slicker that he had indeed killed his mother at the age of three weeks and had also ardently wished for the destruction of the whole human race, but he thought that that wish had not come upon him until he was four weeks old, though he could not swear to it.

"Really?" said Dr. Slicker. He sounded disappointed. "You must be very careful about not giving back to me what I have been suggesting to you. That also, of course, is entirely natural. I cannot search around in somebody's mind without leaving some dirty handprints—I mean a few marks—behind. You have said to me very little about your father and I have deliberately not questioned you in that area. However, knowing now my techniques, I want you to spend several hours thinking of your father and your mother and then see whether you cannot come up with the real explanation of this fantasy you have invented about an elephant called Golden Lotus and being the guest of Dr. Pangloss."

Hari now began to understand the game a little better, for although trusting he was not without intelligence. For the next several days therefore when Dr. Slicker visited him, he said that although he had been thinking very deeply about his father, all was confusion and he could make no sense out of his thoughts.

After two weeks, however, he confessed to the great psychiatrist that he now recalled everything, but was too fearful to relate the full story.

"I am your friend," said Dr. Slicker. "Look upon me as your confessor. Unburden your fears to me and you will be immediately relieved of them and will enter into a newer and fuller life."

"Alas," said Hari, "to speak of what I have found out is to dishonor my own father."

"You owe him nothing," said Slicker. "He is only your father. Therefore tell me everything."

"Sir," said Hari, "my father is a murderer."

"It is often the case," said the psychiatrist, licking the end of his pencil preparatory to taking notes.

"It was not I who killed my mother as I told you the other day. That was a terrible lie and I hope you will forgive me for it. My father was the villain. He came into the hut while I was nursing, took a cutlass and split my mother's head open like a watermelon so that the blood and brains splashed all over me. I have never been able to abide the taste of warm milk since."

"You must not be too hard on him," said Dr. Slicker. "What he did was perfectly natural if we but knew the circumstances. But I must warn you that it is as bad for you to hate your father as it is for you to love your mother. There is no right and wrong in the world. These are old concepts coming out of the dark ages of superstition and religion. There is only behavior. And behavior is neither good nor bad—neither praiseworthy nor blameworthy. It is merely understandable. Unless men come to realize this they will never be truly free. It surely must be quite clear to you that guilt will never be banished from the world unless we first of all cure ourselves of saying and thinking that certain actions are wrong and certain actions are right. Right and wrong are obstacles which men place in the way of free behavior and they must be removed."

"You mean it would not be wrong of me to throw an old woman into a river and it would not be right of a passerby to pull her out and save her life?"

"Quite so," said Dr. Slicker. "The two of you would merely be behaving in a manner which at that time was natural to you.

"But to return to your own case, you still do not quite understand what happened to you. However, now that I have all the facts before me, it is very simple for a man of my training to put them together in the proper order and so discover the kind of psychosis from which you are suffering and the cause of it.

"You have deceived yourself into believing that you think your father was the murderer of your mother, and entertained a deep hatred and revulsion of your father for that reason, but this is not so."

Hari thought for a moment, with sinking heart, that his fabricated tale had been discovered as fiction, and he must therefore endure a further period of being beaten on the mind by Dr. Slicker, but this was not so.

"Now the facts are," the great psychiatrist continued, "that physically your father split your mother's head open with a cutlass and so caused her death, but the guilt of that action you did not lay on your father, but have taken to yourself."

This statement so astonished Hari that he could make no comment on it. None was needed.

"The reason that you took the guilt of that action on your own head, was because you yourself had wished your mother dead. When therefore your father killed your mother, this seemed to you to be the granting of your wish—it seemed to you that your wish was the motivating force behind the murder. And that therefore you yourself were responsible for the deed."

"Because of prenatal heartburn?" asked Hari.

"Precisely," said the eminent man. "Now we come to the retreat to the fantasy land in which you have taken an elephant as a mother substitute and given it the name of Golden Lotus.

"Have you any idea why you should have chosen an elephant as a mother substitute, instead of some other animal—say, a cat?"

"Elephants don't need to be housebroken?" ventured Hari.

Dr. Slicker brushed that aside. "Because it is impossible to split the head of an elephant in two with one blow of a cutlass," he cried. "No other animal would serve except perhaps a hippopotamus, and these are rarely domesticated.

"Now I am pleased indeed to have solved your case. I have to leave you for I have another patient—the top half of an eighteen-year-old soldier who keeps crying for his mother. His legs were blown off by a land mine together with the greater part of his buttocks. You are sufficiently aware of my methods now, I am sure, to realize that he is not crying for his mother for love or affection from her, not from loneliness, nor terror in the face of death, but only because as a child he grew to dislike her and is now suffering from an overwhelming sense of guilt of which I must relieve him."

At that moment the door opened and a meek young man wearing a flower in his hair and completely naked except for a string of beads entered the room without knocking.

"Dr. Slicker," he said, "I have come to thank you for freeing me of the intolerable burden of guilt under which I struggled for so many years of my life. You will never know how wonderful it is to realize that in selling mind-expanding drugs to children at cut prices, thereby causing the deaths of a few score of them and permanently blinding others, I did nothing wrong but was merely behaving in a perfectly natural manner and that it would have been quite unnatural of me to have behaved in any other manner at that time."

"The gratitude of the patient is the reward of the doctor," said Dr. Slicker meekly.

Thereupon the young man produced a machete from behind his back and struck off the doctor's head with one blow. He stared at the twitching body of the great psychiatrist for a while and said, "He really cured me, you know. I haven't got even the teeniest sense of guilt."

Chapter
Eight

LEFT with the body of Dr. Slicker, Hari quickly came to two decisions. The first was that the great psychiatrist was beyond all medical aid, though he would remember him in his prayers. The second was that although Dr. Slicker, true to his principles, would certainly never attach any blame whatever to the man who had struck off his head, society at large would not take so enlightened a point of view. Someone would be held responsible and undoubtedly hanged, and it would therefore be prudent for Hari to leave as early as possible. This he did by slipping out of the window, his room being fortunately on the ground floor of the hospital.

Outside Hari quickly made his way across a few lawns and, mingling with hospital visitors and recuperating patients, passed through the gates and out into the city. He now had but one desire and that was to return to his own village on the banks of the tributary of the Ganges and meet again his beloved Golden

Lotus. Whether she was a mother substitute or an elephant did not matter to him in the slightest degree.

"Oh, if only I were with her again, bathing in the river and hearing the patter of the wind in the delicate leaves of the bamboo, how happy I would be," he cried. "My dear Golden Lotus, you will never know how much I miss you." Indeed the thought of his elephant filled him with such a sense both of nostalgia and of loneliness that he sat by the side of the road and wept.

Several saw him but passed him by, since a weeping man is certainly nobody's business. But a little girl came to him and asked him why he was crying; and when he said it was because he was lonely for his elephant Golden Lotus, she offered him a bite of a mango she was eating. Learning that he was on his way to India, which she understood to be a considerable distance off, and that he had nowhere to stay, the child assured him that he would be welcome at her mother's home.

"Ah no," said Hari. "I am sure your mother has enough troubles of her own without having a stranger bring her more."

"Not at all," replied the little girl. "My mother says every day that nothing pleases her more than when a lonely stranger calls at her house." That there should be such an angel in the world, which up to the present he had found populated only by demons, greatly heartened Hari. The little girl took him by the hand and, leading him down several streets of a mean sort, brought him at last to a house made of sheets of rusting corrugated iron beaten flat. It was, in fact, more of an iron box than a house and instead of a door had before it a curtain made of sacking.

"Go in," said the little girl. "Do not be afraid."

There was nothing else to do but enter, and inside Hari found himself in an atmosphere heavy with tobacco smoke garnished with rancid olive oil. For a while, so dim was the light, he could see nothing. Then he made out a few rags in one corner on which a baby was sleeping, and against one side of the little tin box of a house, a miserable bed on which a young woman was lying.

She woke as he entered, yawned and said, "Give me a hundred piasters and take off your clothes."

Too late Hari realized why the little girl's mother was so happy to meet lonely strangers. He was about to leave when the young woman—little more than a girl herself—grabbed his robe and begged him to stay, saying that she would oblige him in any way that he wished provided he had even as much as one piaster to offer her, or even a piece of bread.

"Alas," said Hari, "I have nothing whatever to give you but the clothes I stand in. I have just come from the hospital."

"You have nothing to fear from me," said the girl. "I have not got the slightest trace of the pox. Are you entirely cured yourself, however?"

Hari explained that he had not been in the hospital for the reasons she thought but because he had been beaten on the feet, shot in the leg, and hung up by his thumbs. This brought expressions of sympathy from her and she inquired what might be his calling.

"I am an elephant boy," said Hari.

"Well," said the woman, "I suppose that every trade

has its hazards, but I think you would be altogether safer working in mine. Little Tatita has not the judgment to know what kind of men to bring here though I expect that later on she will be a greater help to me in finding customers. Also, although she is only five years of age, she shows promise of maturing soon and then will be able to share in the heavier duties of my profession. Will you not undertake yourself to get customers for me when I assure you I will give you one half of what I make?"

"Shameless woman," cried Hari aghast, "do you really use your lovely little daughter to attract men into vice—and would you really train her in so degrading a profession? I will not stay one moment longer in your presence."

"Ah, please do not leave me, sir," said the woman. "Have you nothing whatever you can give me? I can find no food for the baby, and Tatita has been living out of garbage cans for days and from whatever mangoes she can find lying in the gutter."

Hari was about to leave anyway, but at that moment the curtain of sacking was thrust aside, and the woman with one movement threw some horrid-smelling cloth over him to cover him. She spoke in alluring tones to the new arrival, who first of all pretended that he had lost his way, then said he was looking for a friend, then said that it had looked as though it was going to rain and that was the real reason he had entered the house. But the woman coaxed and cosseted him with soft words until he had agreed to three hundred piasters and then a little while later (Hari having remained hidden all this time) announced that he was going but he did not propose to pay her a sou.

"But you agreed to three hundred piasters," said the woman.

"You are nothing but a worthless old whore," said the man. "What you are doing is illegal and if you say one word more to me, I will have the police on you."

Such base behavior so aroused Hari that he threw off the covering under which he had been hiding and, seizing the man, told him that if he did not immediately pay the three hundred piasters he would publicly denounce him as a scoundrel. But the fellow tore himself from Hari's grasp and flung himself off down the street.

"This is the worst misfortune that has come my way since my good father, Son of the Mountain, sent me here to save my life by prostitution," said the woman.

"Is it possible?" cried Hari. "Are you indeed Moon Lily, daughter of Son of the Mountain and Celestial Flower?"

"That is indeed so," said the young woman, "and who are you?"

Hari then explained all about himself and they wept together over the death of Son of the Mountain.

"Alas for my poor mother, Celestial Flower," said the woman. "She will certainly starve now, and if she were only here with me I could in some way take care of her."

"I wonder what day it is," said Hari.

"Whatever has that to do with my problem?" demanded Moon Lily through her tears.

"It might be Mother's Day," said Hari. "In which

69

case all will be well for the Best of All Possible Nations will do anything in the world for mothers on Mother's Day."

Thereupon Hari took Moon Lily and Tatita with the baby to a public pump conveniently located only two miles away and there they washed themselves. He then, having made inquiries, found the BAPN consulate and, having ascertained that, by the greatest of good fortune, it was indeed Mother's Day in the Best of All Possible Nations, politely requested of the receptionist that he see the consul.

Instead of answering his request, the lady gave him a form to fill out. This form was of extreme length demanding his age, nationality, place of birth, parents' age, nationality and places of birth, his residences over the last fifteen years, his reasons for leaving his residences over the last fifteen years, the places he had worked at for the last fifteen years, together with the names of all his employers and the reasons why he had left these places, and left this work; his next of kin and relationship to next of kin and the place of residence of next of kin; whether he was married or single and if married, why, if single, why and if divorced, why; the number of his children, their sex, their ages, the schools they were attending and whether they had ever taken part in any rallies protesting the overseas policies of the BAPN; and a great many other questions so that it took Hari the better part of two hours to fill out the form. However, he eventually got the task completed and took it to the lady, who without a glance put it aside and told him to go to the end of a line that stretched out of the building and several blocks down the street.

"But I only want to see the consul for a moment or two."

"Then why did you fill out this form applying for a passport visa?" demanded the young lady, tearing it up. "Are all you people stupid?"

"Is it possible for me to see the consul?" asked Hari meekly.

"No," snapped the young lady.

"But it is Mother's Day," Hari protested.

This produced the most astonishing effect. The receptionist glanced past Hari to Moon Lily, who had little Tatita at her skirt and her baby in her arms. Then she picked up the telephone and, having dialed a number, said into the instrument, "There is a woman here with a baby. She wants to see the consul in connection with Mother's Day. Yes, sir. I will send them up right away. Yes, sir."

Immediately she beckoned to a messenger who conducted Hari and Moon Lily with Tatita and the baby through the crowd to an elevator in the back of the lobby. Such instantaneous acknowledgment of the sanctity of Mother's Day enormously impressed Hari. He had been affronted by having being made to fill out the form for a passport visa, but though he had not spoken a word about his feelings, he now felt ashamed even to have harbored in the recesses of his mind the slightest hostility to the BAPN.

So as he entered the elevator, wishing to make amends for his uncharitable thoughts, he turned to the crowd and cried in a loud voice, "Be patient, my

71

brothers, for these are truly good people. See how the consul intends to honor Mother's Day by receiving this unfortunate prostitute with her illegitimate children . . ." He got no further, being thrust into the elevator and the door shut, but not before he heard a roar of what he took to be enthusiasm from the crowd in the lobby.

They went up but one floor and were immediately admitted to the presence of the consul.

"You!" cried the consul in astonishment when he saw them.

"You!" cried Hari in equal surprise. For the consul was none other than the man who, having enjoyed Moon Lily's favors, had repented his promise to pay her three hundred piasters and made off without giving her a penny.

"You villain," cried Hari. "You took advantage of this poor mother on Mother's Day and then refused to pay her! Wait until I explain that to the people waiting downstairs."

"You are entirely mistaken," said the consul. "I left in a hurry only because I recalled that I had a most urgent appointment back here in my office. In short, I had to be here to receive the two hundred billion piasters which are sent each month to this country to promote the peace, freedom, security and happiness of these unfortunate people by unremitting warfare."

"Two hundred billion piasters?" cried Hari. "So much?"

"We may increase it to three hundred billions," said the consul with a smirk.

"I beg of you, sir, do no such thing," cried Hari.

"Rather spare the people and send them not a penny more, for I do not believe they will long survive your good intentions."

"It is plain that you do not understand international affairs," said the consul. "Now as to your own private affairs, I think the agreed price was three hundred piasters and I will pay that under protest, for I am getting sick and tired of the exploiting of our people by the citizens of this country, whose liberty we are pouring out our fortunes and our lives to achieve."

"Sir," said Hari, "that is not entirely the reason we are here. As a result of the good intentions of your government, this woman is a prostitute at an age when she should be in school, her child roams the streets looking for clients for her mother, and her mother is starving to death, her husband having been shot by one side or another. Therefore, this also being Mother's Day, I request that you take some of that two hundred billion piasters you have just received and spend it on uniting this woman with her mother and providing them with housing and support other than prostitution."

"That would be misappropriation of funds and I will do nothing of the sort," said the consul. "The whole of that money is earmarked for slaughter."

"It is plain then that you do not believe truly in the sanctity of Mother's Day and that my only recourse is to inform all the people waiting below of your attitude," said Hari.

But this the consul wished to avoid, and so, after a little more discussion, it was agreed that Moon Lily would be put on the payroll of the consul as an aide at a salary of two thousand piasters a month and provided with proper quarters and that efforts would be made to find her mother, Celestial Flower, and unite her with her daughter.

Hari received an advance of salary for Moon Lily amounting to twenty thousand piasters, and it was just as well that he did. For it appeared that his generous words to the people in the lobby had been misunderstood and had resulted in a riot. The mob beat down the doors of the consul's office and would have torn the consul limb from limb if Hari had not assured them that he had settled with Moon Lily and shown the twenty thousand piasters to prove this to be so.

Immediately the attitude of the mob changed. The consul was covered with necklaces of flowers, produced from nowhere, and photographs were taken of him standing close to Moon Lily and Tatita with the baby in his arms. He then became the most popular consul in that country ever appointed by the BAPN. Wherever he went flowers were strewn in the streets before him and people cried out that it was true that he really loved their country and was not ashamed of their people.

Then, to everybody's astonishment, he was recalled to his homeland.

"The truth is," said the people, "the BAPN want only to be hated, and to this purpose they spend billions of piasters a month all over the world. They are sick. Perhaps one day they will have spent all their money, got tired of exerting their authority wherever they go, and we can talk to them as brothers and cure them of their strange illness."

Chapter Nine

WITH the money received from the BAPN consul, Hari was able to find a little home for Moon Lily and Tatita and the baby. Moon Lily insisted that Hari share the home with her (for he had nowhere else to stay) and he began to make inquiries about Celestial Flower. He heard that there was a central refugee office which would be the best place to inquire. But there he found the premises deserted except for an old watchman.

"What has happened to the refugee officials?" he asked.

"They are themselves refugees," said the watchman. "Do not be in a hurry, my friend. You are rushing nowhere but to death. Therefore sit down and enjoy yourself. Be assured that death will come in its own time and will not fail to find you, so why rush around seeking it?"

"I am looking for Celestial Flower," said Hari, and explained the circumstances, for he was above all things a frank and open young man. The old watch-man, whose very bones seemed wrinkled with age un-der the brown folds of his skin, listened to all he said and then assured him not only that his mission was useless but also that he was a fool.

"If you are looking for someone to help," he said, "there are a million people in every kind of wretched circumstance in this city as a result of this madness over democracy. Therefore take your pick of them. But to complicate your task by looking for one particular person to help is the height of foolishness. Consider now—if everyone with a desire to help a friend or a relative, helped instead whoever was nearest to him and in need of aid, then their own friend would be helped, though by a stranger; all wretchedness would quickly disappear from the world; and people would for the first time be truly civilized. I have lived a very long time and what I have told you is the sum total of all my knowledge. It is the basis of a religion called Christianity which is discussed by many but practiced by only a few."

"There is a great deal of wisdom in what you say," said Hari.

"I am glad you think so," said the man. "But wis-dom unapplied is foolishness compounded. Therefore if you do not want to have the name of being the big-gest fool in this whole city, give up your search for Celestial Flower and take me instead to the little house you speak of, for I am completely without support of any kind and in quite as much need as the ugly old woman you are at such pains to succor."

The logic of the old man's argument being irrefu-

76

table, Hari brought him back to Moon Lily, who agreed to feed him if he would, in return, each day bring water from the public pump, which was now only half a mile away.

"That I will certainly do," said the old man, "if you will in return promise me each day two heaping bowls of rice with, mixed in each, a handful of raisins and an ounce of goat meat. Also I must have two piasters a month on which to get drunk and sing the songs of my youth, for though you can find it hard to believe, yet the fact is that once I was a young man."

This Moon Lily agreed to readily, and on the following day she gave him his first full bowl of steaming white rice, with plump raisins and delicious goat flesh in it. The old man ate the bowlful and then called to an urchin playing in the road.

"Boy," he said, "it is plain to see that you are thin and hungry and, being constantly underfed, will not reach the delights of old age as I have done. Therefore you may clean my rice bowl twice a day if in return you will take those two buckets, fill them with water from the pump, which is only a few steps from here, and bring them back."

The boy readily agreed to do this, but the old man, whose name was Hakim, made him first fetch the water.

"Truly riches in the hands of the foolish work no good," he said to Hari, who was about to upbraid him. "See how with as little as a few grains of rice in the bottom of a bowl I am able to help this young man achieve the dignity of labor, improve his physical being, hold out to him the prospect of living to a great age, and provide this household with water."

"You are nothing but a lazy old rascal," said Hari.

"Peace, friend," said Hakim. "What harm have I done you? The boy is stronger than I. He will be able to bring more water. Will the water taste any better if I carry it here myself?"

"But Moon Lily could have given the boy the same amount of rice as you are getting, and received the same work in return," said Hari.

"The difference is that she did not think of it," said Hakim. "Also reflect that nobody can accuse her of profiteering from the young. That sin belongs to me, but I must be paid for committing it. There is nothing in the world that comes free. Remember also that the wages of sin exceed the wages of virtue and are paid in cash or kind."

Hari then, whose mind was always open to reason, allowed the old gentleman to stay; and he proved so astute in his bargaining that he soon had boys vying to carry the water for him, and in fact built up an organization of boys which was ready to do his bidding in any way possible. He used these same boys to find customers for Moon Lily, whom he persuaded not to spend the money she had received but to keep that carefully hidden as a reserve.

As a result little Tatita no longer had to roam the streets seeking lonely strangers to bring to her mother, but was able to go to a good school where she learned that all that her mother was doing was reprehensible, that the old man was a devil and the little boys whom he helped to feed for their services were condemned to burn forever in a pit of everlasting fire.

Being a sensible little girl she learned her ABCs but paid no attention to such fairy tales.

Chapter Ten

HARI discovered that when Hakim had told him that the people who ran the refugee office were themselves refugees he meant that the problem of handling the daily increasing number of refugees had become so enormous that they had had to move out of the city to an area of ground several square miles in extent, in which the refugees were housed. There were several hundred thousand of these people and Hakim thought it highly probable that Celestial Flower would be among them.

"But," he said, "it will be entirely impossible to find her, and that for a number of reasons. First because of the great number of people who are in the same state as herself and with whom she will be herded. Second because she will not be known by her name but by her number. Third because there will be no cross-reference between her name and her number since the Goodies cannot speak her language and so cannot write down her name. Fourth because once anybody is put

80

in the cages in which these people are kept, they entirely lose their individuality and an indivdual can only be found if he or she remains an individual. Fifth because you have no idea of which category she has been placed in, as for instance: Item, a prisoner of war; item, a civilian defendant; item, a civilian suspect of civilian intelligence; item, a civilian suspect of military intelligence; item, an innocent civilian of the first class; item, an innocent civilian suspected of family relationship with a civilian defendant; item . . ."

"Never mind," said Hari. "I will go and look anyway. Take care of things here while I am gone."

So he made his way out of the city and found the enormous city of cages which contained the refugees and which covered an area of several square miles. It was entirely surrounded by an electrified fence reinforced by barbed wire and had been located on the summit of a series of hills so that there was not the slightest natural shade available for those detained there. These were housed in wooden buildings with roofs of galvanized iron, and these structures, which looked remarkably like prisons, stood on ground completely stripped of all grass or other covering, so that when the slightest breeze stirred, clouds of tawny dust drifted all over the area.

A large unpaved road led to a guardhouse which was near a gate through the electrical fence, and behind the guardhouse was a building on which was a sign that, despite the grimness of the whole place, raised Hari's hopes. The sign read "Military Police."

"Surely these must be very good and intelligent people if they realize the necessity for policing the military," he said, and, approaching the sentry, he asked where he could inquire for a missing person named Celestial Flower.

"You got any identification?" asked the sentry.

"Sir," said Hari, "I am only a private person."

The sentry gave a shout and two soldiers appeared from the building marked "Military Police."

"What's the trouble?" they asked.

"Unidentified civilian trying to get into the compound. No papers," said the sentry.

"Come with us, shithead," said the two soldiers, and dragged Hari willy-nilly into the MPs' office.

There he found that the worst sin a man is capable of committing is to have no papers and be near a refugee settlement. In addition to having no papers, Hari had no story that could account for his lack of papers. He certainly was not going to tell his questioners that he was an elephant boy from India and the guest of Dr. Pangloss lest he be submitted to more flagellation of the mind at the hands of another psychiatrist.

He did the very best he could to concoct a credible story, saying that he was seeking Celestial Flower, who had befriended him after the airplane in which he had been traveling had crashed; but even as he was telling this tale he knew that he was not believed.

His questioner was a sergeant who sat at a desk in a negligent manner, leaning back in a swivel chair with his feet resting on the top of a wastepaper basket. He was fat, pink, and fair and had a faint but persistent resemblance to a sweating pig. While Hari produced his tale he was looking out of a window to the side of

82

him in utter boredom. When Hari had done he threw him a piece of paper and said, "Can you write?"

"Yes, sir," said Hari.

"English, I mean," said the sergeant.

"Yes," said Hari. "I was taught English by a missionary who said that all men were brothers but that he was a big white brother and we were little brown brothers."

"Well, write your name on that and where you come from and don't give me any of your lip," said the sergeant.

When Hari had done this, the sergeant got up from his desk, with such effort that it was plain that this constituted in one large action his total day's work, went to a filing cabinet and took out a badge with a number on it.

He wrote the number on the slip of paper on which Hari had written his name and, turning to the two soldiers who had brought Hari in, said, "Civilian defendant. Stick that on him."

The number was thereupon pinned on Hari's blouse, and he was taken by the two soldiers to one of the cages on top of the sun-smitten hill and pushed inside. It was in vain for Hari to protest that although he was certainly a civilian he was no kind of a defendant and indeed he did not know what he was to be called upon to defend himself against.

"You'll find out," was all he was told.

Inside the compound were perhaps two thousand others in the same position as himself. None of them knew why they were there, how long they were to remain or what was to happen to them eventually.

One very old man, his shoulders stooped from decades of work at planting rice and whose name was Ho Fat, assured Hari and all who would listen to him that they were there entirely because of their own fault.

"We were lacking in wisdom," he said, "and so we suffer. We are the mice who, harassed by a dog, were fools enough to summon the cat to our rescue. Now the cat devours us. What is your story, my son? Tell me every detail and be assured that I will listen carefully for there is nothing else to do here whatever."

Hari believed that he could trust the old man and so told him everything, and Ho Fat was very happy with the tale and said that it entirely accorded with the state of things generally and the total condition throughout the world.

"I have long tended to the opinion that the world is run by madmen," he said, "and what you tell me confirms me in this view. You are aware, of course, that this war is being fought entirely for our benefit by the BAPN so that we may be able to pursue, each in his own way, life, liberty and happiness. It is only natural then, the leaders of the world being mad, that you and I should be imprisoned for no reason whatever since what we seek is liberty. It is also only natural that being in search of happiness we should both be made wretched—you by being taken away from your lovely river and your charming elephant and I by being deprived of my wife, my two fine sons, my grandson, my farm, and the graves of my ancestors, which now lie untended if indeed they have not been bombed into oblivion by our well-wishers.

"Now if this were but a casual misfortune which

84

had overtaken only a few people, it would be understandable. But it is the common fate of the people of this country, who, to tell you the truth, never had any hand in the matter in one way or another. Our first leader in this war was shot as a traitor and, with the country swarming with soldiers and all our food dependent upon them, we were asked to vote for a new leader from a number of candidates—one the general who leads the armies and so has complete control over the country and all the food in it and the rest of them people we had scarcely even heard of. Naturally we voted for the general. We thus demonstrated our love for democracy and political freedom to the world and assured ourselves of continued distribution of rice. If I were a young man I assure you I would immediately become a soldier in one army or another. Which does not matter in the slightest for any soldier is safer than any civilian, and with madmen in charge, who is to say that one is right and the other is wrong?"

The old fellow was entirely convinced that the world was run by lunatics who had managed to keep their mental state concealed from the common people. "When they are in danger of being discovered, they go to war," he said. "All reason or use of reason being abandoned in time of war as dangerous to the nation, they are then entirely safe."

"I think that I see a flaw in your reasoning," said Hari. "I will grant you that Germany's war against France was the act of a madman. Also Japan's war against America was the act of a madman. But the present war from which you suffer surely cannot be the act of a madman since it was not brought about by either Japan or Germany."

"Son," said Ho Fat, "I hope you will pardon me. I have made the mistake of starting to think. It is a weakness of old age which I trust you will overlook."

Ho Fat's own story was a mere variant of that of everyone else in the cage to whom Hari talked. He had been planting rice in his fields, which were surrounded on each side by hills rank with growth. There had been a few rifle shots but he had become accustomed to these and paid no attention for they seemed some distance off.

Then a group of soldiers had come splashing across his rice paddy and had passed him. They went into the opposing series of hills and he again paid them little attention for it seemed to him that planting rice was more important than watching soldiers.

After a little while three of the soldiers came back to him and one who could talk his language asked him three questions.

"What were they?" asked Hari.

"My name. The village I came from. And why I had not taken any notice of the shooting."

"And what did you reply?" asked Hari. "For your reply must undoubtedly have awakened their suspicions."

"Quite so," said Ho Fat. "I told them my name was Ho Fat, that the name of my village was Tenji Bijik Manarattis Degi Hotoranuk, which means Place of Peace by the Temple of the Purple Bamboo, and the reason I had taken no notice of the firing was that I had a great quantity of rice to plant that day.

" 'Ha,' said the one who could speak my language (I am ashamed to say that he is one of my countrymen), 'that is the clue. He was planting rice as a signal to the enemy that our patrol was in the neighborhood.' And so I was arrested and brought here as a civilian defendant."

"And what does that mean?" asked Hari.

"I must prove that I was planting rice to plant rice, and not planting rice to kill soldiers," said Ho Fat.

"That will be very difficult," said Hari. "In time of war it seems that planting rice or any peaceful activity is a very suspicious occupation."

After he was arrested, Ho Fat said, he was not allowed to return to his wife to tell her what had happened or even to put the unplanted shoots of rice in a shady place to save them, for it seemed that they also were under some kind of suspicion. They were flung on the ground to die in the sun, and a burlap sack was put over his head so that he could not see where he was being taken to.

He was marched in this condition a great distance, often falling down and being poked and hit by rifles. Then he and a number of other suspicious planters of rice were put into a truck with the burlap sacks over their heads. They heard rifles being cocked and believed that they were going to be slaughtered; but this was only the Goodie soldiers having a little joke with them, for soldiers see little fun in their lives other than drinking, killing, obeying orders and violating women, and are entitled to their idle amusements.

From the truck they were taken to an airplane and made to sit on the floor. They did not know it was an airplane they were in as none had ever been in such a contrivance before. They knew only that suddenly whatever they were in began to rise rapidly in the air with a great roar and scream and their ears hurt them with an intensity of pain beyond description so that they cried out.

The soldiers laughed at this, finding it very funny indeed, for a few split eardrums among rice farmers is nothing whatever to concern the troops of a civilized nation. Also they looked very funny with their heads and shoulders covered with burlap sacks, screaming with pain and banging at their ears. They were then landed, given numbers, and put into the cage and Ho Fat had been there ever since.

"Have any been released?" asked Hari.

"Yes," said the rice farmer. "There is one sure sign that a man is to be released. He is given a clean pair of trousers. There is some hope that those to whom clean pairs of trousers are given are not shot, for that would seem a great waste of trousers. Indeed this is what buoys up most of my fellow prisoners, and when we pray at night we pray as follows: 'Great and Magnificent God, of your mercy and goodness send me, if it is your will, a clean pair of trousers tomorrow. Amen.' "

"I will include that among my own prayers together with the prayer that God will permit my elephant Golden Lotus to have a calf," said Hari. "For even if I should die but Golden Lotus has a calf, then I would know that all is not lost in the world."

"God will hear you, my son," said Ho Fat. "He delights in these prayers offered for others—even for elephants. Your Golden Lotus must truly be a magnificent creature."

"No. She is not magnificent," said Hari. "But she has a kind heart."

Chapter Eleven

THE prisoners in the civilian defendant cage—
indeed the prisoners in all the various cages at what
was called the Refugee Camp—were supplied with
food by the Goodies and the food, they were assured,
was of the highest nutritional value and came from
the biggest food companies in the Best of All Possible
Nations.

It consisted of tomato paste, dried onion soup, and
spaghetti which was itself liberally smeared in its can
with tomato paste. The can when opened smelled like
the heart of water buffalo three days dead. To this
there were added cans containing strange tubes of meat
called sausages or franks, but few would eat this for
the meat was unidentified and religious scruples prevented some from eating the meat of the cow, others
the meat of the pig, and yet others the meat of the
monkey. The mystery of what these tubes of meat contained was solved, however, by one of the prisoners who
could speak a little of the language of the Goodies.

90

He told his fellows that one day, when he had been called to work in the kitchen of the Goodie soldiers, one of the soldiers had opened a case containing cans of these tubes of meat and had said, "Horseshit. Goddam franks again." Horseshit, he explained, was the Goodies' word for the excrement of horses.

A few among the prisoners decided that they would sooner eat horseshit than blood from the stale hearts of dead water buffaloes poured over the intestines of eels, and none believed when they were told that the food with which they were supplied was the best obtainable and eagerly eaten by the inhabitants of the Best of All Possible Nations. A few had, in the early days, petitioned to be given their own food, which was rice and dried fish, but they had been told that that was pig food and inferior and they must raise themselves above such lowly fare and learn to eat the superior food of the BAPN.

The change of diet produced severe stomach pains among the greater number of them, so that they were sure they were being poisoned. However none died of the food, but Hari himself suffered excruciating stomach pains in his first three days as a civilian defendant and longed heartily for the *roti* of his native land, however inferior it might be to the food of the BAPN. Thereafter he recovered his health slowly and, fortified by his custom of prayer, which gave him the strength of someone who does not feel himself alone, hoped that a new pair of trousers would one day be sent for him.

In the early part of his imprisonment he expected that Moon Lily or Hakim might come looking for him, but after a little reflection decided that they would not do so for both would undoubtedly, having no papers, be soon in the same cage with himself; and in the days that followed, there being nothing whatever to be done in the compounds, he often discussed with Ho Fat the significance of papers and the relative importance of papers as compared with people.

"It seems to me," said Hari, whose disposition was always entirely good-natured, "that after all, the BAPN in insisting that everybody have papers are doing this only for their good. They intend that nobody shall ever be overlooked or confused with anybody else; that each shall be able, through the system known as papers, to preserve his individuality and be recognized by a number as he would by a name. After all, it is possible to confuse similar names, and so mistake one person for another and attribute to the one the misdeeds of another. But with numbers, that is to say with papers, this would not be possible."

"Your youth and natural generosity are leading you into error in the matter," said Ho Fat. "And let me caution you, before proceeding, that I may also be leading you into error as a result of my age and my tendency to think, which I am now unable to control, and so I will never be happy again.

"With that warning in mind, I would like to suggest that papers are given in the belief that through them it will be possible to control people. What happens is this. There is a man who represents himself. And there are papers that represent the man. Now if the man says one thing regarding himself and the papers say another and different thing regarding him, then there is a conflict. Do you follow my reasoning so far?"

"It is all quite clear to me up to this point," said Hari.

"Good. Now in a conflict between a man and papers, the word of the man will not be given credit, for it may properly be held that the man is biased in his own behalf. But papers cannot be biased for they have no feeling one way or another and therefore what a man's papers say will be believed and what he says himself that is contradictory will not be believed."

"But how can there be any contradiction between the papers and the man? Surely the one must be but the true reflection of the other."

"Ah, what happiness to be young and what a curse to be old!" cried Ho Fat. "Once I myself had such innocent thoughts and the world was a delight to me. But to address myself to your question. What is your true identity?"

"I am Hari Rinjit Singh, an elephant boy from Ramapore, which is a village on a tributary of the Ganges."

"Your papers say that you are No. CD 184 297 233 zsp, a civilian defendant," said Ho Fat.

"But that is a mistake which will be rectified."

"That is a mistake which *may* be rectified," said Ho Fat. "The point is that because of a paper written by someone who is not yourself, you are here. And the power of the paper is such that you will remain here until the paper is altered—by someone other than yourself. Not only you but all the people in these cages numbering many thousands. All are under the control of a paper which is the superior to them, individually and collectively.

"Now there is something in this which is subtle and mystical and it is this. Paper is more powerful than man. Therefore paper is superior to man. Therefore the fate of each man depends on his paper. Therefore in the new theology of the Best of All Possible Nations (for once they worshiped God even as you and I do) God is now a document and lives in a machine from which he issues his commands."

"But this would make them pagans and idolators," said Hari.

"That is true," said Ho Fat. "Once I believe they knew God, but now they have for the most part lost Him. It is for this reason that they are becoming mad."

Later that day Ho Fat came to Hari and said, "I believe I am to die. There is a cowbird which has been sitting on the fence for the past three days during the noon hour and looking at me and it is a fact beyond dispute that all birds bring bad news. This bird flew three times over my head and then plucked a hair from my scalp and that is its message—that I am to be killed."

Nothing Hari could say would comfort the old fellow, who begged Hari to gain possession of his body and take it back to the village of the Place of Peace by the Temple of the Purple Bamboo and lay it beside those of his ancestors. "Although you are not of my religion," said Ho Fat, "yet my God will smile on you for this act of kindness and will bring blessings to you all your life. Also when you are dead, as much water as can be held in the blossom of a sacred lily will be

94

brought to comfort you each month among the fires of Hell."

"Why are you so sure that I will go to Hell?" asked Hari.

"God is merciful," said Ho Fat gently, "but who can forgive a man for eating goat flesh?"

Hari took no offense at this remark for the Holy Sadhu Punjat Tremor Raki had assured him that no man should condemn the religion of another unless he had personally questioned God on the subject. Also he was quite sure that Ho Fat was sincere in his views and it was kind of him to think of sending a lily blossom of water to him in the distress of Hell.

But seeing Ho Fat so downcast at the prospect of dying, and being unable to shake his belief that he was to be killed, he hit upon a scheme to raise the old fellow's spirits.

"If I become you and you become me, then, I being under no threat of death, you will escape," he said.

"But this can only be achieved in another life," said Ho Fat, "when it is true I may be born again as a rich rajah or even a captain in the army of the Goodies, who are without a doubt the most powerful men on earth."

"Not at all," said Hari. "We have only to switch numbers, for remember that now you and I are numbers and not people as we used to be when we were on the other side of this cage."

After a little persuasion, Ho Fat agreed to this, and the two men exchanged numbers with each other. That very evening Hari's number (that is to say Ho Fat's) was presented with a new pair of trousers and the following morning a man in a uniform came to him, shook him by the hand, gave him a candy bar, explained that all had been a mistake and he was free to go wherever he wished.

Delighted to be at liberty, Ho Fat rushed from the enclosure out into the road, where he was struck by a speeding truck and instantly killed. A cowbird circled over him piping mournfully as he lay in the dust.

Hari, on the other hand, was informed in the same hour that he was to be shot for planting rice in a peaceful manner, thus deceiving a patrol of the Goodies into believing that there were no enemy forces in the neighborhood.

"But I am not whom you take me for," he cried when informed of this sentence. "I am an elephant boy from India and the guest of President Pangloss."

"We have your number," was the reply. "Are you going to argue with that?" And he was put in a truck to be taken out to the place of execution.

Chapter Twelve

In the back of the truck were two other unfortunates also going to their execution. They were dirty
and unshaven and their hair was matted and they were
clad in the clothing of the peasants of the countryside.
They seemed unconcerned about their fate, however,
for they were playing cards with a deck which had
passed through many hands and were so intent on their
game that they scarcely gave Hari a glance as he was
pushed into the back of the truck with them.

"Fifteen-two, fifteen-four, fifteen-six, fifteen-eight,
two's ten, two's twelve and nibs is thirteen," said one.
"I got to take a leak."

He looked around and saw Hari prostrate in one
corner of the truck, saying his prayers.

"Son of a bitch," he said, "it's that goddam elephant
boy."

"Sam!" cried Hari, forgetting his devotions for the
moment. "Bud! Where have you been? What are you

doing here? I thought you were both killed in the plane crash."

"We're going to be shot. What about you?" asked Sam.

"I'm going to be shot too," said Hari.

"What for?" asked Sam.

"Planting rice in an innocent manner," said Hari. "And you?"

"It is a short story and soon told," said Sam. "How we survived the plane crash I do not know except that the plane, coming down in a rice paddy, did not catch fire or rebound into the air when we would have been killed. We were both knocked out by the impact, however, and when we came to, found the plane buried in the mud of the paddy with only a part of the tail assembly sticking out. We of course were trapped, and I expect would have died inside of starvation but a patrol of the Baddies found us. They blew a hole in the end of the plane with a grenade and we crawled out.

"In our service we are required to destroy all our identification if captured by the enemy and this of course we had already done. So we had no papers. We were then subjected to the most terrible tortures to get us to reveal who we were . . ."

"But nobody would believe you?" interrupted Hari.

"Correct," said Sam.

"You said you had come to get an elephant boy for President Pangloss?"

"No," said Sam, "we weren't that stupid. We said we were insurance salesmen."

"They beat you on the feet?"

"Unmercifully," said Sam and Bud together.

98

"And only when you told the lie they wanted to hear were you believed?"

"Precisely. We said eventually that we were warplane manufacturers, trying out a new plane, but that we repented our evil ways and were willing to do whatever we could to make amends. We were then immediately enrolled as volunteers in the army of the Baddies. We had to take part in several raids and when finally we were captured by the Goodies, it was only natural that we should be condemned as traitors. It's a big mess, but it will all be tidied up nicely in half an hour when we're shot. Who would have thought that when we first met by that river in India, we would wind up being shot together?"

"Something of the sort happened to Sinbad the Sailor," said Hari. "But not on account of his lacking papers," he added. "I had never realized how dangerous it is to be without papers. And now I will never again see Golden Lotus, nor learn if she had a calf, nor listen with her in the summer silence to the whisper of the bamboo in the south wind." And at the thought of the separation, Hari burst into tears and neither Sam nor Bud could console him.

At last they arrived at the place of execution. They were taken from the truck and made to stand before three upright poles to which they were tied with their hands behind their backs. A squad of soldiers formed some distance off in line and at attention. The officer in charge of the firing squad, standing a little way in front of the three men, read to each of them, with some difficulty, the order sentencing them to death and the reasons for the sentence. His difficulty arose from the fact that he had never managed to pass a reading readiness test and was, in fact, never ready to learn to read. That he was then an officer should surprise no one.

"Have you anything to say?" he asked of the men.

"I regret that I have failed President Pangloss," said Sam.

"I regret that I have failed President Pangloss," said Bud. "And this is the last time I'll vote Democrat."

"I regret that I ever heard of President Pangloss," said Hari. "And I would like you to give my respects to your twin brother."

"My twin brother?" cried the officer, blanching. "What do you know of him?"

"I had the honor of making his acquaintance in the psychiatric ward of the city hospital when he lopped the head off Dr. Slicker," said Hari.

This little exchange, delaying the execution for perhaps a second or two, nonetheless saved Hari's life and that of his companions. For hardly was it over when a truck appeared a great distance off but raising a boil of dust as it roared toward the execution party. The officer would have taken no notice of it but proceeded with his duty since there was nothing in his orders to say that he was not to shoot the men if a truck appeared. However, his soldiers managed to delay a little in preparing their rifles and complained that with the noise the truck was making they would be unable to hear the order to fire. So the order for the killing volley was delayed until the truck had arrived. It pulled up by the squad, enveloping them, the officer and the condemned men in a cloud of dust which only gradually

100

subsided, so that all disappeared and then slowly reappeared as if resurrected from the grave.

"What's all this about?" demanded the officer when he could at last see the truck driver.

"The war's over," said the other. "Here's a paper which says we are to stop firing. I guess that includes you."

"You're kidding," said the officer. "Who won?"

"You're kidding," said the soldier. "Who cares?"

The members of the execution squad immediately lost all discipline, threw down their rifles, ran to the condemned men and, cutting them loose, assured them fervently that they had never wanted to kill them and hated the whole business and embraced them and gave them chewing gum—this being the ritual peace offering of the Goodies. They then all piled into the truck to go away; but when Hari, Bud, and Sam asked to be allowed to accompany them the officer produced a piece of paper which said that military vehicles were for the sole use of military personnel and civilians riding in them would be subject to the severest penalties, not, however, to exceed death.

"In that case," said Sam, "we'll walk, for I do not wish to join the army just to get a ride into town. And in any case I could not, not having any papers."

So the three companions, the dust of the truck's departure having died down, walked happily back to town to be united with Moon Lily and Hakim and with a good prospect that Celestial Flower, now that the war was over, would be released from whatever limbo she occupied and be reunited with her daughter and grandchildren.

Chapter Thirteen

Hari had but one ambition now, and that was to return to India as quickly as possible and, having found Golden Lotus, never leave her again. Moon Lily completely sympathized with this desire and proposed to pay his fare out of the twenty thousand piasters she had received from the BAPN consul who had been recalled for being too beloved of the people.

"For I certainly owe all my present happiness, my growing clientele, my little house to you," she said. "If at some future date," she added, "you should desire any other companion than Golden Lotus (whose charms I do not for one moment discount) then I hope you will bear me in mind. As you know, I am a good cook, and can launder clothes very well, and am proficient in other activities though overusage has perhaps taken away the keen edge of my natural ability there. That, however, would return with rest."

Hakim counseled against spending any part of the money in this manner. "Nothing is as valuable as accumulated capital," he said. "Once got together, always with tremendous difficulty, it should never be spent for any other reason than to bring an increase. Thus it may be lent but only on consideration of interest. It may be invested but only on guarantee of a return with interest. It may be used to accumulate property but only if the property has more value than the price paid. If it is spent for travel, the travel must produce more than the price paid (which is certainly not the case in returning our young friend to India). In short it is a sin against commerce, and a sin of the most grievous kind, to part with capital except for ample profit.

"If you will excuse my saying so," said Hari, "I find it strange that you should know so much about the use of money, for I believe you are the poorest man in this city."

"Once I was the richest man in this city," said Hakim, "but was ruined by hypocrisy."

"In what way?" asked Hari.

"It was very simple. At the start of the war which has, alas, just ended, when I was quite a young man, I obtained through bribery a post as a storekeeper with the government. Many other posts were available but I wished only to be a storekeeper of the lowest grade since I knew that in this position lay my greatest chances for enrichment.

"You are aware that every war brings with it a tremendous importation and movement about of goods of every kind. All these goods, starting perhaps with mere millions of dollars' worth, and increasing to billions of dollars' worth as the war reaches its inevitable stalemate, must pass through the hands of storekeepers, and that then being my position, I was able to watch the flow of this huge and increasing tide of treasure into the country and around the country.

"I came to know which items were needed where and which were needed in a hurry. By slightly delaying the delivery of critically needed items I was able to call attention to the fact that a small payment to me would speed them up in the future. When no payment was made the items were lost; that is to say, they were removed from the storehouse and sold in what is called the black market, fifty percent of the price received returning to me.

"It was not long before it became known that although only a storekeeper of the third class, I was the man to see when any particular item needed finding. And since my superiors were engaged in the same trade they certainly never thought to complain. Many times I was offered advancement because of my efficiency in releasing critically needed goods when the conditions required for their release had been met—or finding whole trainloads of goods which had become lost in some warehouse where they were not supposed to be stored. I always refused these offers of advancement, preferring to remain out of the public eye, where I had the opportunity of taking my profit or blackmailing my employers.

"However, they, by their greed, brought the whole government into disrepute, though I had been preparing for this. A reform group seized power, the Prime Minister was shot as a corrupt traitor and war profiteer and I went immediately to the reformers and gave de-

104

tailed evidence concerning my superiors, causing many of them to be shot and others imprisoned for life. As a mere storekeeper third class, living very modestly in the meaner part of the city, I was not myself suspect. Indeed, I retained my post and, when all had settled down, began once more to delay delivery of a shipment here and lose trace of a shipment there and so on. And then the blow fell.

"I had expected the reformers, as reasonable men, to continue the game which they had interrupted. But instead I was seized and investigated; relatives of those against whom I had testified now testified against me and, in short, I was utterly ruined by the hypocrisy of the reformers. From the richest I became the poorest man in the city."

"Hypocrisy?" cried Hari. "It was you who were the hypocrite and they who were the honest men."

"Not at all, my friend," said Hakim. "For when they had seized all my assets and utterly ruined me (I was permitted to go free for having informed on my colleagues), they themselves turned to the same sport. But each man, if he would profit from experience, must look within himself for the answer to his failures and not go blaming others for his own faults. And the answer to mine is plain indeed. In dishonesty I was a past master. But I had not studied hypocrisy sufficiently to survive in government."

Hakim then opposed paying Hari's fare to India and Bud and Sam would hear nothing of it. Having been since the crash of the airplane in the hands of the military on one side or another, they had been kept away from all civilian authority. They now approached

105

the new BAPN consul and revealed to him who they were. He declared that he had had the whole intelligence service at his disposal looking for them for the past several weeks.

"Ah," said Bud, "then no wonder we weren't found."

The consul immediately arranged for an airplane to take Bud, Sam and Hari to the capital of the Best of All Possible Nations, where Hari would meet with Dr. Pangloss at last.

"First, however," said the consul, "you will have to pass our health and immigration inspections."

"But I have already passed them," said Hari.

"Since you have not got the paper to prove this, you will have to pass them again," said the consul. "Just step into the next room and take down your pants."

Chapter
Fourteen

WHEN Hari arrived at last in the capital city of the Best of All Possible Nations, he was astonished at the reception which was accorded him. He was met at the airport not only by President Pangloss but also by many members of the President's cabinet, by generals of the army and admirals of the navy and high officers of the air force, and by several members of the diplomatic corps of countries neighboring India.

A score of flashguns were held aloft and exploded in his face, microphones were put before him in thickets and television cameras were aimed at him from every angle. He was formally welcomed by President Pangloss, who beamed on him a smile of radiant friendship, put his arm around him, squeezing his tetanus shot, and informed the microphone hedge that all his life he had wanted to meet an elephant boy from India and now that ambition had been realized and he was sure that nothing but good would result. He said that the confrontation between East and West for a man-

107

to-man exchange of views was essential to the peace of the world. He said his wife agreed with this view.

He said it was important for people in an expanding world, which was at the same time contracting, to learn as much as they could about each other, their lives and their methods of earning a living. He then gave Hari another squeeze on his tetanus shot. The microphone was then put in front of Hari and he was told to say something. He said that although it wasn't easy to become an elephant boy he would do his best to teach President Pangloss the rudiments of the profession. It took a long time living with an elephant to be able to work with it and elephants very often took a dislike to their masters and would not do anything that was required of them. The microphones were then cut off.

There were many hundreds of people at the airport to see Hari arrive and be received by the President. Some of these carried placards saying: "Pangloss Forever," "Peace with Pangloss," "Pangloss Is Best." To these the President waved and smiled. "It is good to be beloved of the people," he said. But from a certain section of the crowd came catcalls, whistles and rude noises.

"Take no notice of them, my dear Hari," said the President. "Some of our people, I am afraid, don't like foreigners."

On the way to the President's palace, President Pangloss asked Hari whether he had had an interesting journey. "Yes indeed," said Hari. "I escaped from a plane crash, was dragged through the mud by my feet like a dead man, beaten on the soles of my feet until

108

I fainted, hung by my thumbs, forced to invent a story that my father had murdered my mother to preserve my sanity, imprisoned for not having any papers, and finally condemned to die before a firing squad."

"That reminds me of something that happened when I was a little boy," said President Pangloss. "We came of poor but honest folk and I used to have to walk ten miles to the little red schoolhouse over rough country to get my education. One day I noticed I was wearing a hole in my shoes, so to save my mammy and my pappy some expense I took them off and walked barefoot. I got a splinter in my foot but I didn't say a word to nobody. I consider the Free Boots for Rural Schoolchildren Bill one of the most important measures before the present session of the Congress."

This remarkable reply led Hari to believe that President Pangloss had so many problems on his mind that he did not really hear what was said to him, and that he made conversation out of politeness and was not really in search of information. He decided then to relieve the pressure on the President by keeping silent, but the President himself insisted upon talking, at times asking him questions and at times undertaking to explain various matters.

"One of the most precious of our freedoms," President Pangloss said, "is the right to protest. This, of all things, we must safeguard against any attempt at restriction. At the same time, it is important for the people to realize that when the President is right, it is wrong to protest his decisions and his actions. In fact to use the power of protest when I am right is to abuse the power of protest, and abuse of that power will eventually lead to weakening it. Therefore those who protest against me when I am right are weakening the sacred right of dissent, which is the foundation stone of the strength of our nation, and are therefore weakening the nation. It grieves my heart to see them taking away from their children that which they hold most precious for themselves. It follows then that there should be no protest unless authorized by the President, for the protest against the President when the President is right is a willful obstruction to the work of the nation.

"This," he continued, "may be a little difficult for you to follow being a foreigner. But it should all be crystal clear to any voter in this country with a grade-school education."

"If I may be permitted a question, sir," said Hari, "I would like to know when the people may be sure that you are right—so as not to protest or oppose your actions?"

"Why, that's simple," said Pangloss. "I never do anything unless I'm right and I never say anything unless I am sure of it. It follows therefore that protest, in my case, can be equated with disloyalty to the whole of our system. I consider the Bill Requiring the Opposition to Show Cause before Exercising the Sacred Right of Protest in Time of Crisis one of the most important measures before the present session of the Congress."

Chapter Fifteen

URING the days that followed President Pangloss set aside a little while each evening to instruct Hari on the methods of government in the Best of All Possible Nations and the principles which underlay these methods so that when he returned to India he would be able to explain the whole system to his countrymen.

"The underlying principle is freedom," said the President. "Each individual has certain inalienable natural rights and to insure that these are not taken away from him, the Congress each year passes about four hundred laws, and then each of the fifty provinces into which the country is divided has its own congress. They in turn pass laws, some of them as many as seven or eight hundred a year. Below these are counties which are administered by boards of elected officials called commissioners and these also pass laws, and side by side with these are the cities of which we have more than any nation in the world.

"Each of these cities has its own government which also passes laws and there are also schoolboards and planning commissions, health authorities, road commissions, harbor commissions, communications commissions, pension boards and hospital boards—all of them making laws and rules designed to insure the greatest degree of liberty and happiness for each individual under their jurisdiction.

"Indeed I believe that I can truthfully say that in this great nation of ours the individual citizen is the subject of more lawmaking than in any other country in the world. Whatever his needs we have a law covering it, and our legislation is so complete and so farseeing that it takes into consideration what may be the Happiness Demand Potential of the citizen ten, twenty or fifty years from now.

"As, for example," continued the President, scarcely drawing a breath in his enthusiasm for the subject, "you have undoubtedly heard the saying that money is the root of all evil. Now in a nation of increasing prosperity there is a rising danger to the whole population that they will accumulate money in excess of their needs and lay up stores of this substance to the ruin of themselves, their families and ultimately the nation.

"Therefore we have devised a plan whereby the more money people earn the more money is taken from them, and this plan is now approaching the point where it is quite impossible for the greater part of our citizens to save any money at all. Thus they are in very little danger of accumulating any of this monstrous source of evil."

112

"But if they are unable to save money, what happens when they become old or sick and are unable to work?" asked Hari. "I know that in a nation as advanced socially as yours their relatives do not take care of them."

"True," said President Pangloss. "But we do have Mother's Day and Father's Day, and Christmas Is For The Children. Don't forget that. But to answer your question, it is quite true that in sickness and old age people are without savings to take care of themselves, and so the government takes care of them. The sick, on proving that they are sick, are given a small check and medical care and the doctor's bills are paid by the government eighteen months (in some cases longer) after presentation. Also those too old to work are given a pension, but care has to be exercised to see that the pension is not such as encourages the individual to idle away his old age in luxury."

"How is such a judgment made?" asked Hari.

"In general if the old-age pensioner is found to be keeping a canary or has bought a book in the past year, he or she is brought in for questioning," said the President. "We find that in all but the most stubborn cases the canary is dispensed with and the habit of book buying discouraged.

"From this you will see," the President concluded, "that in our nation the government is deeply concerned with and enters into every aspect of every individual's life, from the cradle to the grave. In my next budget message to the Congress I am going to try to extend this care by asking for the establishment, under the health department, of a Bureau for Preconceptual Aids to Children."

"Preconceptual aids to children?" echoed Hari.

"The duty of the bureau would be to visit all newly married couples and according to their economic circumstances, genetic inheritance, voting record and party affiliation, tell them whether they should have children or not, thus relieving them of the responsibility of making this decision themselves. As you know, it would be a distinct advantage to some children not to be born at all, and only the more old-fashioned of the philosophers (now utterly discredited) will maintain that life in itself is a gift beyond all value.

"Our Department of Health and Welfare has statistics to show that below a minimum income of two thousand dollars a year and one bathroom for every three occupants, children are better dead. Also children of Low Income Potential Parents are better sterile since they will otherwise only produce Low Income Potential Children. We cannot indefinitely continue as a High Income Potential Nation with a Low Income Potential Population. A cut has to be made somewhere."

"I know that you have given a great deal more study to these matters than I," said Hari. "So I trust you will overlook my ignorance and forgive me making a comment which is made not from rudeness but out of surprise."

"It is a free country," said President Pangloss. "Our legislators at every level are working by the thousands day and night to make it freer. Therefore make any comment you want."

114

"You have said, sir," said Hari, "that you have statistics to show that under two thousand dollars a year income, children are better dead. Yet, I assure you, Mr. President, in my country there is not one family in a hundred that earns two thousand dollars a year."

"Ah, the burden of the backward peoples of the earth," said President Pangloss. "You have no conception how heavily it weighs upon us. It deeply grieves my heart. However, we have plans to change all that. Under a cultural exchange agreement which is presently being worked out teams of experts will soon be sent to your nation to make the people aware that they are unhappy.

"They will be made to see how selfish it is to bring children into the world to run about naked in the sun and splash in puddles of water in which the germ count must be appalling. They will be made to understand that they are utterly wretched in having to live in little villages enduring the cycle of the seasons when they could live in air-conditioned homes unconscious of winter or summer, their mental capacities fully developed by a modern education so that they can engage their minds in the works of civilization—such as developing clean hydrogen bombs instead of merely milking cows.

"Believe me, I am saddened when I think of the sufferings of the backward nations of the world and the appalling waste they represent. There are I believe four hundred million people in your country."

"As to that," said Hari, "I do not know. Nor do I know how anybody knows since it is impossible to count such a large number of people. For many would have been born and many others died by the time the count ended. But in my village there are three hundred and thirty-seven people and according to our good Sadhu three gods, five water spirits and a sacred snake."

"We can change all that with one bulldozer and we will, for we are your friends," said President Pangloss. "But what are we to do about four hundred million people all engaged in agriculture? Problems of this kind keep me awake at night. My wife too."

This was but one of many conversations Hari had with President Pangloss, who in all emphasized that the underlying principle of government of the Best of All Possible Nations was the pursuit of life, liberty and happiness through the medium of saturation legislation at all levels of control.

"And, of course," the President said, "always bear in mind that anyone who can think of a new level of control is making a very real contribution to the security of the people. Life being, by its nature, full of hazards and unexpected happenings, it follows that the more control we have, the less are the hazards and the greater the happiness of the people. Full control in every area is then the only guarantee of full happiness in every area. I want to be known as the President who brought the greatest happiness to the people by making the government a fully participating partner in every one of their activities.

"It would fill my heart with joy if, every night, on going to bed, I could be assured that each citizen of this nation said, 'Good night and God bless you, dear President Pangloss.' "

Chapter
Sixteen

Hari, a few days after meeting with President Pangloss, ventured to take up with him the war in Sasia which had but recently come to a close.

"I am glad indeed that you have decided to touch on this important matter," said President Pangloss. "This has certainly been the most misunderstood effort to promote happiness in which we as a nation have ever engaged. It grieves my heart to see the extent to which we have been defamed in this venture."

"What was the object of the war?" asked Hari. "Nobody in Sasia seemed to know."

"You see the depth of the misunderstanding?" said President Pangloss. "Even you, an honest elephant boy from another country, are affected by it. It was not a war at all. That is a libel—a deliberate lie. It was a peace program."

"How strange," said Hari. "It looked remarkably like a war. I saw soldiers using flamethrowers, grenades, howitzers, mortars, machine guns, rifles, bayonets, airplanes and tanks. Also people gutted, bifurcated, beheaded and torn apart by these same weapons. Also villages stinking with dead, and women and children barbecued to a turn—sometimes en brochette for the women were holding the children.

"I assure you, President Pangloss, that it looked so much like a war to those involved in it that they are to be forgiven if they did not know that it was, as you say, really a peace. But would you kindly excuse my ignorance and tell me how one may distinguish between the two, for when I was hanging up by my thumbs, being beaten on the feet, thrown into prison and put before a firing squad, I really thought these things happened to me because a war was raging."

"The difference is twofold," said President Pangloss. "If our nation is attacked, then it is my duty as President under the Constitution to consult with the Senate, and if the Senate votes by a two-thirds majority that we should defend ourselves—then it is a war and is so proclaimed. However, if some other nation is attacked or some other nation says that they are attacked, and they ask us for help, then it is not a war but a breach of the peace and so I, as President, do not have to consult the Senate but can send all the troops I can get and spend all the money the Congress can be persuaded into voting to help those who need help. In this case, as you will see, it is a peace program, for what we seek to do is not to wage war but to restore peace."

"What a pity Celestial Flower did not know of this when her sons were killed, and Ho Fat too and all those others who were imprisoned with me," sighed Hari.

"If they had realized that their anguish was caused by peace and not war, perhaps it might have consoled them."

"And who is Celestial Flower?" asked Dr. Pangloss, and Hari explained about her.

"That reminds me of something that happened in our own little town when I was a boy," said President Pangloss. "There was an old widow who had three worthless sons who were finally all jailed and the old lady was left without any support. However, our Garden Club held a champagne and caviar supper for her benefit and we collected twenty dollars which was presented to her at a public function by our mayor, who happened, at that time, to be up for election."

"And what did the old lady do with the money?" asked Hari.

"She bought a gun, shot the mayor, the president of the Garden Club and then herself," said Dr. Pangloss. "It is easy to see where her sons got their own criminal natures. It is not always easy to help people, as you see. Nor is one always thanked for it."

After some days of personal instruction President Pangloss finally suggested that Hari would benefit if he were to meet some of the more influential members of the Congress. Hari, deeply impressed by the sincerity of President Pangloss but entirely puzzled as to how an increasing multitude of regulations could promote freedom of the citizens of the Best of All Possible Nations, was himself anxious to meet some of the legislators. He was then put in charge of a presidential aide with instructions to take him first to Senator Tot-

119

tering, Chairman of the Senate Foreign Relations Committee.

"Perhaps you are unaware," said President Pangloss on parting, "that in our nation promotion to the heads of the important Senate committees is entirely by seniority. The oldest senator heads each committee, and the oldest senator of all is Chairman of our Foreign Relations Committee since this is the one we consider most vital to the security of our beloved country. This system insures that each committee is steered by the senator with the greatest experience and wisdom.

"These venerable senators are of course above political considerations for their re-election becomes a matter of habit, and they have therefore no ax to grind. They are able then, without the slightest bias, to decide what matters should be put on the agenda of their respective committees for examination and after examination be put before the whole Senate with a recommendation for voting.

"Senator Tottering, whom you will soon meet, has been a member of our upper house for well over fifty years and his wide and deep experience in foreign affairs, through almost three generations, is of tremendous value in the framing of our policies."

"And is this excellent policy followed in all professions and occupations?" asked Hari.

"Not in the least," said President Pangloss. "You are not to conclude that because a man at ninety-two is fitted to take a leading part in directing our foreign policy, formulating our fiscal program, examining our tax structure, recommending the extent of our educational expenditure and proposing rules and regulations for our national communication and our involvement in space and other scientific research he is to be trusted to drive a bus. Nor is a man who can propose the expenditure of two billion dollars a month in public funds to be allowed to operate an adding machine or work as a door attendant or run a garbage truck. In all these occupations, and indeed in every other activity of our great nation, men are compelled to retire at sixty-five. It is only in government that those in power are entitled to go on forever."

"And at what age are your citizens permitted to vote?" asked Hari.

"Not until they are twenty-one," said President Pangloss. "By which time the greater number of them have already served their compulsory periods in the Army, Navy, or Air Force which they must do when eighteen. To permit them to vote earlier might result in the abolishment of the Army, Navy, and Air Force. Young people are very hotheaded and our survey shows that no man will support a war if he has to go to fight in it himself."

Following this little explanation President Pangloss sent Hari on his way with the presidential aide, who soon took him over to the Senate Office Building after he had first consulted a directory to see where it was.

Senator Tottering was in his office, reclining in a chair of black leather. His face was so enormously aged that it was hard to discover from looks alone whether he was alive or mummified. His figure resembled what was earlier called an anatomy of Death, and he did not stir in the slightest when Hari was brought in and introduced to him by the Senator's secretary, a

121

spry youngster of seventy or so, and in fact his younger brother.

"Speak to him through the microphone," said the secretary. "The Senator has a cold in his ears and is a little hard of hearing this morning."

But appearances in this case proved entirely deceptive for the Senator was by no means moribund. He fixed Hari with an ancient and glittering eye and in a high falsetto hissed at him, "Millions for defense. But not one cent for tribute. On that I take my stand."

"This gentleman, Senator," said his secretary, "is here bringing us greetings from India. He is the guest of President Pangloss and comes to you to learn something of the function of your powerful department."

"The Dey of Algiers is a damned rascal," snorted the Senator. "So is the Bey of Tunis and the Yusuf of Tripoli. Pettifogging, silk-clad, luxury-loving goddam foreigners. I don't know who your master is, young man, but he is probably the same and you can take back to him that message I just gave you in reply to your demands—millions for defense but not one cent for tribute. Here. Have someone write it down."

"India," said his secretary. "India, Senator. India. The gentleman is from India."

"Tippecanoe and Tyler too," snorted the Senator. "On that I will stand or fall."

"The Senator often falls into these reminiscing moods," said the secretary. "In a sense he is part of his nation's history and the past is as real to him as the present. Sometimes he likes to roam through the centuries before coming to the crises of the moment, but his tremendous background never leads him astray.

122

Sir, this gentleman is from India and brings you greetings from his great country."

"Let me tell you something about India," said the Senator, now thoroughly animated. "I've been thinking about India and I've been studying India. And I've come to this conclusion: no country where the people have to stand on their heads to think and haven't yet got around to inventing the musket is ever going to amount to a row of pins. Now if you ask me where the enemy is I'll tell you—Africa."

"The future of the emerging nations of Africa is a matter of concern to the whole world, Senator," said his secretary.

"Emerging nations be hanged," rapped the Senator. "Keep an eye on that confounded Dey of Algiers."

After this outburst the Senator concluded the interview by falling either into a coma or asleep—it was impossible for Hari to decide which.

"You had better leave now," said his secretary. "He has a very busy day ahead. There is a serious quarrel among the lamas of Tibet which must be very closely investigated. The Red Hats claim that the Yellow Hats have stolen one of their scrolls, and supporters of the Red Hats are infiltrating the grounds of the Yellow Hats, who have, very naturally, appealed to us for help. This matter will occupy the Senator in hearings which are to open this afternoon, and in the meantime four squadrons of heavy bombers have been alerted to be ready to preserve the peace. You do not by any chance speak Tibetan, sir?"

"No," said Hari.

"A pity," said the Senator's secretary. "We shall have

to hold the inquiry and decide the issue without any-one being able to speak a single word of their language. Still, it has been done before and many times."

The presidential aide accompanying Hari said that his name was Cy Rush, that he was a graduate of the University of Chicago in philosophy, of the University of California in business administration, of Harvard in law and London in economics. He was a young man and his university studies and flat feet had prevented him from serving in the Army as did other young men not similarly handicapped. After leaving the univer-sities he had obtained a number of positions such as packing automobile tires in a rubber plant and being stockkeeper in a pottery manufactory, crossing guard at a major intersection in a small town, cashier at a hot dog stand in Coney Island and inspector of dog licenses in Hermosa Beach, a small town in Southern California.

Having failed in all these occupations, however, he had turned naturally to politics and there his success had been brilliant.

"I organized a public opinion poll and sent my find-ings weekly to every radio and television station and newspaper of importance in the land," said Cy. "These findings were so outrageous that no one would pub-licize them. However, when the votes were counted I was found to be entirely right and so came to national prominence and was quickly appointed a presidential aide because of the accuracy of my forecasts."

"And what were your findings that they should have been considered incredible?" asked Hari.

"My findings were that Dr. Pangloss would be elected President of this nation," said Cy.

"But surely, if Dr. Pangloss was so unpopular, the results of your own poll would have indicated that he would not win," persisted Hari.

"My poll was unique in that I refrained from polling," said Cy. "I had learned at the university and in my various careers that the public will do exactly the opposite of whatever the experts predict. This is true also of the stock market. Therefore all I did was examine the various other polls, which asserted confidently that Dr. Pangloss could not win, and reversing this, make the prediction that he could not fail to be victorious. My prediction was accurate to within two percent of the vote."

"And do you conclude from this that public opinion polls are an important factor in influencing the outcome of elections?" asked Hari.

"I conclude from this that public opinion polls are a national amusement like dowsing for water, that all the public wants is peace and employment; that every candidate promises this so there is nothing to choose between them; that the left side of President Pangloss' rival's face did not photograph well on television, and President Pangloss was therefore elected because both sides of his face are symmetrical and he likes dogs. But here we are at the office of Senator Glory, Chairman of the Committee on Patriotism and one of the watchdogs of our nation. You will learn more from him about our country than from any other one individual, Dr. Pangloss excepted."

Chapter
Seventeen

"Patriotism," said Senator Glory, "has been described by a foreign writer as the last refuge of a damned scoundrel. The very words condemn the man who is known otherwise only for having compiled a highly inaccurate dictionary. I will give you now a definition of patriotism in words which will burn into your mind and remain there forever. Are you ready?"

"I am indeed, sir," said Hari, eagerly awaiting so magnificent a pronouncement.

"Patriotism is unquestioning, unhesitating, and the fullest obedience to the government of your country—I mean my country—and the principles for which it stands. Patriotism brooks no quibbling. It tolerates no hesitation. It permits no second thoughts. It demands complete, uncomplaining and enthusiastic obedience. And it follows then that your true patriot, sir, is the fairest blossom of the nation's manhood, compared with whom all others are but weeds."

"But, sir," said Hari.

"What do I mean by the principles of our country, you are going to ask?" demanded the Senator. "I answer you that they are written out in a fair hand for all the world to see.

"The principles of our country are devotion to freedom in all its forms—freedom of speech, freedom of the press, freedom of the pulpit and from the pulpit, freedom from unwarranted arrest, freedom from unwarranted search and seizure, freedom in short in every glorious and God-given activity of man." He paused to wipe the corner of his eye with the cuff of his sleeve.

"And what do I mean by government?" he continued. "By government, sir, I mean the supervision by the properly constituted authority of every activity of every citizen of this nation to insure that he uses these freedoms in such a way as to promote the welfare of his nation as a loyal son, and of his fellow citizens. And it is in this important area that my committee is called upon to do its vital work. No loyal citizen of this country can ever be shown to have suffered in the slightest degree by testifying before this committee as is the duty of every loyal citizen called upon to do so. Indeed, many who have testified have been amply rewarded by public confidence and positions of affluence in the motion picture, television, and other industries which mold our public thought, and reflect our public image.

"But when someone comes before our committee with mistaken and personal concepts of his rights—when someone comes before us who is using his rights in such a way as to threaten the rights of his fellow citizens, then it is our duty to examine him and expose him as a nonpatriot and thus an enemy of the nation."

"But, Senator," said Hari, "surely if all have the right of free speech and free press, then a citizen who speaks against the government or the system of government has as much right to do so without punishment, as a citizen who supports the government and the system of government."

"Since you are a foreigner you do not understand what freedom is," said Senator Glory patiently. "But perhaps you can understand that there is a difference between a patriot and a traitor. And you will not expect any government, even one as tolerant as ours, to extend to the traitor the same rights as are extended to the patriot. Governments have a right and indeed a duty to preserve themselves and in so doing to preserve their people and the rights of their people. And to fail to do this would be to betray the people and to fail in the prime requirement of government."

"So in saying that all your people have these freedoms, you mean that all the people who are approved by the government have these freedoms," said Hari.

"Young man," said the Senator, "without agreeing with that analysis I want to point out to you that the government is the best and sole judge of who is a patriot and who is a traitor. And you must surely be aware that no true patriot will ever question the actions of his government. In short, sir, all our citizens may be as free as they want provided they do not start asking unpatriotic questions.

"Now as for those who have been before our committee and have been punished, they include a scientist who refused, on humanitarian grounds, to make a bomb that would wipe out half the earth. He failed to see that as a humanitarian government we would never use such a bomb and his refusal to make it was then interpreted as doubting the humanitarian ideals of our great country. A doctor of divinity who demanded that a prayer of some kind be said in our schools and that children be taught that it is sinful to steal, lie, and murder one another; a veteran of two world wars who . . ."

But whatever was the fault of the veteran, Hari never learned. For there was a tremendous tumult in the corridor outside, a great thumping and banging on the door and three men in uniform entered, each carrying a gun and showing signs of having scuffled with the Senator's staff.

"That's him," said one of them. "Grab him."

Before the Senator could say a word he had been handcuffed and struck a blow on the head with a club by one of the uniformed men for good measure.

"What is the meaning of this outrage?" demanded the Senator as he was dragged from his office by his assailants.

"You are under arrest for defrauding on your income tax, investing in foreign munitions industries, misappropriating public funds, and bribing the chairman of a federal investigating agency," said one of the guards.

"All that is true," cried the Senator, "but I have never done anything in the slightest degree unpatriotic. I defy you to prove that I am not a one hundred percent loyal citizen of this great republic."

Chapter
Eighteen

OUTSIDE, Hari, accompanied by Cy, found a vast multitude of people swarming by every approach road toward the Senate Office Building. The multitude was so vast that it seemed that several oceans of people, borne on a powerful tide, were washing up to the steps of the building. Hari immediately concluded that the people had assembled in this manner to protest the arrest of Senator Glory, of which word had undoubtedly spread through the city.

"Stay here," said Cy. "I must return immediately to President Pangloss and report the arrest of the Senator."

"Do you think there will be a riot?" asked Hari.

"Not if I can get to Dr. Pangloss' personal papers first," said Cy, and was gone.

The multitude which advanced slowly on the Senate building carried banners and placards stating their grievances and objects, and Hari was puzzled to find that they bore no relationship whatever to the arrest of Senator Glory. Instead they read: "No Vote—No Draft," "Old Enough to Die—Old Enough to Vote," "Don't Gag Your Son and Then Shoot Him," "No Vote—No Fight."

"Good-for-nothing lousy hippies, flower children and draft dodgers," said a uniformed man standing next to Hari. "Unpatriotic no-goods. Not worth the powder to blow them to Hell."

"What do they want?" asked Hari, who was not aware of the full significance of the various placards he could read.

"Sons of bitches want to take over the government, that's what they want," said the man. "Copulate like rabbits. Never did a day's work in their lives and want to keep out of the Army." He drew his club and started to tap the palm of his hand with it in a nervous and expectant manner. Looking around, Hari saw that a great number of these uniformed men had now assembled and were being joined by soldiers.

"Are they going to attack?" Hari asked.

"Wish they would," said the man. "I'd split a few skulls for them."

"Sir," said Hari, "these people do not seem to me to be more than children—at best very young men and women. Have you no children of your own?"

"I have a daughter whom I love very much," said the man. "And if I found her in a mob like that, I'd beat her brains out."

The vast crowd had now advanced to the steps of the building. They made no noise and carried no weapons though Hari was happy to see that many of them wore garlands of flowers. They flowed quite gently up the

131

steps to the terrace before the building and then, to Hari's surprise, sat down.

No one raised a fist or shouted a word in anger at the uniformed men, who were some kind of armed police, or at the soldiers who had reinforced them. When they were seated one among them got up and, speaking through an improvised loudspeaker, addressed them as follows:

"We have come here to protest, peacefully, the situation in our country in which young men of eighteen must serve in the Army though denied the right to vote until twenty-one. They are therefore gagged and made to fight in wars in which they have no say. We are told that we are too young to vote at eighteen but we are not too young to be killed. We are told we are too ignorant to vote but we know that at eighteen we have more education than our fathers had at thirty. We are told that it is our patriotic duty to fight in our country's wars. But we know also that it is even more our patriotic duty to vote in our country's elections. They will give us a gun but they will not give us a ballot. We want ballots as well as bullets and that is why we have come here."

"Sounds like an incitement to riot," said one of the guards.

"Inflammatory speech on government property and menacing the members of the Congress," said another.

A captain of these armed guards now appeared and addressed the multitude through an electrified bull horn. "You people are trespassing on government property, holding an illegal assembly, and creating a

132

disturbance. I'm going to give you three minutes to get out of here."

"Sir," said the young man who had addressed his followers, "you are mistaken. We have a permit to assemble here and are offering no violence to anyone."

"Your goddam permit don't include sitting on the grass and busting up the rose bushes and giving me any lip," said the guard captain.

The young man turned to address his followers. "The government is concerned about the grass," he said. "You must move off it."

"Three minutes up," said the guard captain. "Okay, boys. Let's go and get them."

The guards thus addressed moved into the multitude, still sitting on the steps, and working in teams of two or three, grabbed people by arms and legs and dragged them up the steps into the building. No resistance was offered them but the guards took the opportunity of beating those they dragged away with their clubs and Hari was horrified to see two or more standing over a young girl and beating her on the head, face and breasts with their clubs while the blood streamed down. The girl cried out, "I'm not resisting. Please don't beat me." Her cries seemed only to increase the enthusiasm of the men with the clubs.

Hari flung himself at one of the guards to protect the girl and was himself immediately seized and beaten to his knees. Before he was dragged away, he saw a guard strike the young girl in the womb with his club and shout, "I'll see to it that you don't have any pups, you bitch."

A large cloakroom had been put aside to receive the

133

captives, Hari among them, who were kicked and clubbed some more and then made to lie on the ground while a man stood over them with a revolver pointed at their heads in case of resistance. Many were bleeding profusely; they had had teeth knocked out, lips and cheeks split open by clubs or scalps bared to the bone by blows.

Some of the girls were crying in hysteria and some threw up on the floor from a sense of outrage. A number had had the clothes torn off them which seemed to please the guards. More and more were brought in, some still defiant and terrorized. Among them was the young man who had addressed them all through the loudspeaker. His nose was broken, his lips split, his mouth full of blood and one eye so badly swollen that it looked not like an eye but a coincidence of plums.

The captain of the guards now came in and, glancing enraged about the room, said, "You goddam cowardly draft-dodging sons of bitches. We'll teach you to respect your country and obey its laws."

"We know now not to sit on the government grass," said one.

"You shut your head or I'll shut it for you," said the captain.

"We have a new definition of a coward," said the leader of the protesters. "It is someone unarmed who is beaten up by someone with a club." For this he was knocked to his knees with another blow. They were left then under guard for some time, during which Hari made the acquaintance of many of them. He noted one thing about them immediately and that was, despite his strange dress, his bloodstained turban and his rent clothes, his dark skin and small build they accepted him immediately and nobody asked him if he was a foreigner.

They seemed in fact to think that he was exactly precisely like them and indeed completely a member of whatever community or cause they represented. Accustomed to being beaten, for he had scarcely traveled anywhere without being brutalized, he was not particularly concerned about being beaten further and assumed that it would inevitably occur. But he was concerned in that he had no papers with him, knowing that, grievous as was his offense in attempting to stop the girl's being clubbed, it was as nothing compared with the offense of not having any papers in the Best of All Possible Nations. He confessed to Chuck, the leader of the protest march, that he had no papers and was very concerned about this but Chuck replied merely that that was "groovy."

"None of us has any papers," he said. "In fact we don't believe in papers. We differ from the authorities in that we believe in people instead."

"And is that the cause of all this?" asked Hari, who had thought that the massacre resulted from the young people sitting on grass which was in some manner sacred.

"No," said Chuck. "The cause of all this is that we are attempting to achieve a change which has never before taken place in any civilized nation."

"And what change is that?" asked Hari.

"We are attempting to give those who must hazard

their lives in a war, a say in whether the war should be fought in the first place."

"This does not seem to me to be so outrageous an idea," said Hari.

"It is contrary to all the rules of civilization," said Chuck. "Admittedly among barbarous peoples such as the Watusi, the Ashanti, the Fijians before Christianity, the Nagi and the Anthropophagi of New Guinea, whoever carries the spear may also vote. But it was quickly seen among civilized nations that this was a culturally degenerate state of affairs since to kill a man is by no means as serious a matter as allowing him to vote before he is twenty-one. Any man of sense can quickly see that there is a mighty difference between a twenty-year-old pilot blowing up a whole city and that same pilot being allowed to cast a ballot.

"The city may be blown up. It is a small matter. But so sacred is the right to vote that the ballot may not be cast until the voter is twenty-one—even if he can claim to have been trusted with the job of blowing up a score of cities of whom the majority of the inhabitants were themselves voters."

"I am afraid that this does not seem logical to me," said Hari.

"And that is the reason why we organized our protest meeting."

Their conversation was interrupted by the reappearance of the captain of the guards, who shouted for silence and then said he had a personal message to read them from the wife of President Pangloss.

Even those with broken jaws, smashed ribs and permanently damaged eyes fell silent so as to listen to the message. It was:

"I very much regret the disgracefully rude and vulgar behavior of many of our young people in our capital city today. A great number of flowerbeds containing roses which belonged to the whole of the people were trampled, grass was torn up over public lawns and the public footpaths covered with an indescribable litter. It will cost your government ten thousand dollars to repair this savage damage. I hope you are proud of what you have done. I am not. Signed, Dovey Pangloss."

"They certainly ought not to have dragged them through the roses," said Chuck. "It would have been just as easy to castrate them by dragging them up the stairs."

After a little while an effort was made, under the direction of the captain, to sort the various prisoners into two classes—those who would be formally charged in court and those who were to go free. This selection was made on the basis of age, sex, race, body weight and condition—a standard which Hari presumed was part of the democratic process. Thus an underweight, young girl, with her face bruised or cut and one or both eyes closed by blows and her vagina bleeding from being kicked, was permitted to go free. But a large older man whose face was unscarred though he had heavy unseen body bruises was led off to be formally charged with disturbing the peace, unlawful assembly, and trampling on the grass and roses.

When the captain came to Hari, Hari's concern about not having the proper papers on him was immediately dispelled. "Get this coon out of here," snapped the captain. "And if there are any other niggers in here, get them out too. We just want whites."

"Why?" asked the guard who was making up the list of those who were to be tried and those who were to be freed without trials.

"We don't want to turn this into a race issue," and the captain. "That's why. Now get on with it."

And so Hari, having learned about foreign policy from Senator Tottering and about patriotism from Senator Glory and about the right of protest and assembly from the clubs of the government guards, was set free to further investigate, if he wished, the conduct of affairs in the Best of All Possible Nations.

Chapter Nineteen

IT was now twilight and cold damp began to ooze over the city from the nearby river. Hari found himself in the vast grounds that surrounded the legislature of the Best of All Possible Nations. His face was bruised, his head wrapped in a bandage, and his clothing torn. He had a vague idea that the presidential palace lay to the north and, taking his direction from the final glow of sunset in the west, set out to find a road leading to it. He had reached such a road as the sun set; and, this being the appointed time for prayer, he faced his sacred city and, prostrating himself on the sidewalk, said the appointed prayers, not forgetting to include his petition that Golden Lotus might be blessed with a calf. As he finished he was aware of a truck stopping by the sidewalk and a man getting out. He turned to see a stranger in working clothes standing over him, the driver of the truck.

"You hurt?" he asked.

"No, sir," said Hari. "I was saying my prayers."

The stranger made no comment, but gathering from this and his clothing that Hari was a foreigner asked him if he had anywhere to spend the night.

"I am a guest of President Pangloss and was staying at the Presidential Palace," replied Hari.

This produced no surprise in the driver of the truck, who remarked only that he had read about Hari in the newspapers. "However," he said, "President Pangloss has left the capital by plane to attend the funeral of the Postmaster in Chief of Upper Arrid in the Persian Gulf who died only two hours ago of a bomb explosion."

"I did not know that Dr. Pangloss was so attached to the Postmaster in Chief of Upper Arrid," said Hari. "He never mentioned him to me."

"On his way," said his new friend, "President Pangloss will stop in England to see the Archbishop of Canterbury, the Prime Minister and the King; in France to see the Head of the Freemasons and the President of the French Republic; in Italy to interview the Pope and the head of the government; in Israel to see the Chief Rabbi and the Prime Minister; in Egypt to see the dictator and the Grand Mufti; in Ethiopia to see the Emperor and the Patriarch; in Pakistan to see . . ."

"Stop, stop," cried Hari. "Surely all these places are not on the way to Upper Arrid."

"They are on the way that President Pangloss will take," said the other.

"And what will he talk to all these important people about?" asked Hari.

"That is, of course, a secret," said his friend, "but sources close to the President—that is to say, his head

140

gardener and the chief bartender at the Press Club—
say that he will talk to them about the unwarranted
cold-blooded, cruel, merciless, callous, and premedi-
tated assault of the Red Hat Lamas of Tibet on the
Yellow Hat Lamas on the trumped-up charge that the
Yellow Hat Lamas, who have always been devoted to
the democratic way of life, stole a certain scroll containing sacred writings from the Red Hat Lamas.
Without wishing to interfere with the internal affairs
of any nation, the President has, after consulting with
his advisors, ordered five divisions of assault troops to
move into the support of the Yellow Hat Lamas. In
short, we are now at war with the Northern Red Hats
of Tibet and President Pangloss is seeking support for
our stand."

"God forbid," said Hari. "Surely not at war again?
The war between the Goodies and the Baddies in
Sasia is only just finished."

"You do not know President Pangloss well if you
do not realize that his guiding precept is 'The Price
of Peace is Unending Warfare.' "

It was then decided that Hari should spend the night
with his new friend, who said he was a farmer from
outside the city and whose name was Joe Trier. He
said he was fifty years of age and had a wife and three
children, all of whom would be happy to make the acquaintance of a visitor from a distant land.

This proved to be entirely true for Hari, since leaving his own country, had never been more warmly received than by his new hosts. Mrs. Trier immediately
assigned him a room in their house and bandaged his
head without inquiring how he had obtained his hurts

141

(leaving him to explain this when he wished) and her husband found comfortable clothing for him to wear while his own was being washed.

The three children were overjoyed at such a visitor. Their names were Joe, Ted and Penelope, Joe and Ted being eighteen and sixteen years respectively and Penelope seven. Before dinner Mr. Trier said grace, which surprised Hari for this was the first time he had heard anyone pray in the Best of All Possible Nations, and during the meal he told them such parts of his story as he thought fit in the presence of children.

Penelope was overjoyed at the thought of Hari owning an elephant, particularly an elephant with so delicious a name as Golden Lotus, and questioned him closely about her. She had herself, she said, a pig called Susan whose manners were a delight and who, when coaxed, could whistle a little song of a certain charm through her nose.

In this house Hari, for the first time since the start of his travels, felt safe and no longer alone.

"I hope you will not judge our nation on all that has happened to you," said Mr. Trier. "The greater number of us live just as we do—some richer and some not so well off. We don't intend any harm to anyone and we like to help others if we can."

"Do you think, sir," said Hari, "that your country was right in supporting the Goodies against the Baddies in Sasia?"

"I don't know a thing about it," said Mr. Trier. "About the time it started I had two sick pigs and twenty acres of corn infested with borer. Later there was an investigation into the whole cause of the war and I obtained a copy of the published results. I committed the summing up to memory. It was easily the clearest part of the report and it went as follows:

" 'It will be seen that the proclivities of the Plin Phlam Phlat regime deriving from the anti-ancestral republicanism tainted with a specious form of quasi-nature worship, itself deriving from the cult of the bamboo weavers (southern Meliong fisher folk of the Instit Delta Region) was antithetical to the infra-structure of the supra-fabric of the Phlat Phlam Plin matriarchal cult with Buddhist outgrowths on the lower level. Complicating this confrontation was the infiltration of Sesemoidic disturbances from synaptic Hinduism imported by the mystic flour-bag manufacturer Doo Ding Dong. Alerted to this danger, the government felt it its duty to send half a million troops to the area and spend two billion dollars a month to restore stability in Sasia and peace to the world.' "

"And you yourself, sir?" asked Hari. "How did this affect you?"

"One of the pigs died," said Mr. Trier. "The other recovered and we lost about six acres of the corn to borer. The trouble with the pigs was swine fever and that was caused by their shelters being old. I hadn't the money to rebuild them but got a government loan."

"A government loan?" said Hari. "That is certainly something to be said in favor of your government that it loaned the money to you for this purpose."

"They loaned me two hundred dollars," said Mr. Trier. "That same year they took nine hundred dollars from me in income tax. That money I had to borrow from the bank."

"And this present war against the Red Hat Lamas?" said Hari. "What are your feelings on the subject?"

"So far the pigs are all right," said Mr. Trier, "but we must have rain in the next two weeks or I shall lose a third of my corn crop."

Hari spent the next several days as a guest of the Triers and enjoyed the quiet solidity, good humor and sense of the household and also working on their farm. He helped to weed in the corn field, to fertilize the potato crop, to pick early peas and clean out the hog pens. In this work he had as his instructor Mr. Trier, who confessed to Hari in discussing voting rights that he did not see that it made any difference whether he ever voted or not.

"If I voted I would be but one of thousands of voters sending one man to our legislature," he said. "Now in the lower house of the national legislature there are one thousand such elected members. Therefore at the national level my vote counts for one two-hundred-millionth part of the whole, which is an amount so infinitesimal that it would be ignored by all but scientists.

"If the matter is put in another way, one thousand legislators represent a nation of two hundred million people, which is so absurd that I wonder anyone takes it seriously. On the other hand, if the national legislature were to be increased, say, to a hundred thousand members, then it would become so clumsy an organization that it would be difficult if not impossible

144

to get them all together to consider any important measure.

"The fact of the matter is that since the first days of our nation, everybody in it has become of less and less importance in each generation. It follows that the only sensible thing for me to do is to attend to my farm; for while I can try to cure pigs and weed corn, I have no influence at all in the quarrels between the Goodies and Baddies, the Red Hats and the Yellow Hats."

"This is truly remarkable and a wonder scarcely to be believed," said Hari. "For I was of the opinion that it was because of you and people like you that Son of the Mountain was killed, that his son was burned alive, that his farm was destroyed, that his wife was forced to starve without shelter in her old age, that his daughter became a prostitute, that I was hung up by my thumbs, that hundreds of farms have been destroyed, scores of villages burned to the ground with liquid fire, and hundreds of thousands of rice farmers imprisoned as civilian defendants."

"I have had nothing to do with any of these things," said the farmer. "And if I met any of these people in need, I would take them into my home and treat them exactly as I have treated you."

"Then Ho Fat was right in his opinion and the world is indeed run by madmen," said Hari. "And you are right in that there is nothing we can do about it but tend to our gardens."

Chapter Twenty

HARI remained for over a week with this pleasant family, who, he concluded, would certainly be welcome visitors in his own village. He became a great favorite of Penelope's, and he told her many fairy tales as, for instance, the story of the Oyster That Trapped a Hippopotamus and the story of the Descent of the Four Ascending Mountains and the story of the Spider That Shook the World. And she in turn told him of many wonders such as Goldilocks and the Three Bears, Little Red Riding Hood, and the difference between C plus and B minus on her report card.

Then one day there was a knock at the door and there stood Sam, the agent of President Pangloss whom Hari had not seen since he came to the country. They had the warmest reunion and Hari explained to Sam all that had happened to him and how the Triers had taken him in. And Sam took down their names and their addresses and Mr. Trier's social security number and Mrs. Trier's social security number and inquired if Joe had registered for service in the Army and at what place and what was his classification and where was his card, and whether Mr. Trier had filed his income tax and also his estimated tax for the current year and for the coming year and paid at least seventy-five percent of the estimated tax for the current year and twenty percent of the estimated tax for the coming year, and also whether they had ever been fingerprinted, and where, and when was the last time, and what was the purpose, and whether in the course of fingerprinting they had objected to being fingerprinted, and if so for what cause, and whether they had ever applied for a passport and if so when and why and whether it had been granted or refused, and whether they had at any time contemplated leaving their country and their reasons for leaving the country, and how much money they had spent abroad and what they had purchased and many other important matters which the government required to know in order to protect their freedom.

When all this was done he told Hari that President Pangloss had been searching for him anxiously since his return from the funeral of the Postmaster in Chief of Upper Arrid. And so Hari was obliged with many regrets and no few tears on both sides to leave his friends and return to the President's Palace.

When he got there Dr. Pangloss greeted him warmly in his study and asked him what he had seen and done in the Best of All Possible Nations. And Hari explained how he had seen a Senator arrested for cheating on his income tax and a number of people beaten for protesting at not being able to vote and trampling

147

on the roses and how he had himself been severely clubbed and then thrown out and taken in by the Triers.

"That reminds me of when I was a boy," said Dr. Pangloss. "I came of a very poor family, though honest, and we never had enough money for me to pay the initiation fees to join the Boy Scouts and buy my uniforms. But I helped so many old ladies across the highway that ran close to our house that our neighbors all took up a collection, paid the fees for me and bought me my uniform as well. And that all goes to show that in this the Best of All Possible Nations anything can be achieved if you just try hard enough and never give up."

"Also if you don't trample on the grass," said Hari, but President Pangloss was not listening.

"The time has come," said President Plangloss, "for you and me to part though it will be with the greatest regret on my part and I assure you I will never forget you as long as I live. And if I should ever visit your country, which I trust I will in the very near future, be sure that I will not fail to get in touch with you."

Hari said he would be sorry to leave also but that he was getting anxious about Golden Lotus.

"The fact is, my dear friend," said Pangloss, "the arrest of Senator Glory on charges of income tax fraud, which I am sure are entirely political, have led us all to examine our financial relations with the government more closely and I find that there is some doubt as to whether you are a tax deductible item. Fond as I am of you and of the emerging and underprivileged people whom you represent, who will always be close to

148

my heart, nonetheless I cannot afford you as a guest if you can't be taken off my income tax. Perhaps you would be good enough to address the Congress tomorrow, which might provide me with grounds for deducting you as a business expense, and then I will arrange for your return to your own country, which I have no doubt you are longing to see again."

Hari was overjoyed to hear this and so the following day found himself addressing the Congress of the Best of All Possible Nations on the subject, "How Your Aid Has Helped My People." This subject had been assigned to him by the Foreign Office in consultation with Senator Tottering, who had said it would be helpful if Hari put in a word or two of caution about the Dey of Algiers. Since he had nothing whatever to say under either heading, Hari ignored them both and spoke as follows:

"I am a very young man and am a member of a nation almost unknown to you. I am too young and too ignorant of your affairs to give you any advice myself and I believe that you are also too young and too ignorant of our affairs to give us any advice either.

"Lacking experience, then, I can only repeat for you the precepts formulated by the Sadhu Panjat Tremor Raki of my village, who is said to be three hundred and fifty years old and who may therefore be worthy of attention.

"These precepts are: Charity begins at home and virtue likewise. Clean your own floors before you find fault with your neighbor's mantelpiece. There is no such thing as 'us' and 'them.' There is only 'we.' Peo-

149

ple who insist they are right are usually merely being wrong in a loud voice."

This was acknowledged by one and all to be the dullest and most futile homily ever delivered to the Congress, which, when Hari had departed, voted an initial expenditure of a hundred million dollars to send schoolteachers to India to replace the sadhus, who plainly had the people in intellectual bondage.

That very afternoon, having signed certain receipts for President Pangloss connected with the President's tax situation, Hari was put on a plane to return home. With him came Sam.

"Are you coming all the way with me?" asked Hari.

"Yes," said Sam. "And I'm not coming back. I've got an air-conditioned home with a twenty-five-year mortgage, three television sets, five telephones, eight suits, a deep freeze, a refrigerator, a concealed bar, several hundred books selected for me by a book club, charge accounts at nine major stores, two automobiles, eight gas cards, five flight cards, sick leave with pay and holidays with pay, hospital insurance, life insurance, fire insurance, automobile insurance and a good job with retirement pay and a pension plan, a credit union, government old age pension, membership in six clubs and a prepaid cemetery lot and I'm miserable."

"You had better come with me indeed," said Hari, "and talk to the Sadhu. But, tell me, are you not married?"

"Married and divorced," said Sam. "My former wife is head of our Parent-Teacher Confrontation, our Growing Girl Group, Child Psychology Action Center, Bureau for Alert Children, Bureau for Exceptional

150

Children, Women's Political Action Committee, Women's Organization to Eliminate Sexual Dimorphism, Women's Shopper's Bureau, Women's Child-Mind Molding Committee, Better Babies Bureau and Mother's Help Institute. On each of these groups she serves on two or sometimes three subcommittees and each subcommittee has meetings with other subcommittees and then reports to the parent groups on which she serves, which themselves also have meetings with other parent groups and then report to the national groups to which she is often a delegate."

"And have you no children?" asked Hari.

"None," said Sam. "When she came home she slept in a separate bedroom and in any case did not wish to become actively involved in motherhood since it might affect her academic standing as an advisor on every area of child activity. She thinks that babies should be fed from overhead sterilized plastic piping containing milk heated by radiant energy and the temperature controlled by thermostats. It is her view that breasts are superfluous and God made a mistake in thinking of them."

"It is the mercy of God then that she is not God," said Hari fervently, thinking of Moon Lily and a certain way she had of standing in the doorway of her little house at twilight, which he now realized filled him with the pleasantest fancies.

The plane on its journey to India landed for fuel in the capital of Sasia; and here Hari was surprised to find even more soldiers, trucks, tanks, military planes, flamethrowers, machine guns, mortars, and cannon than there had been during the recent war. Indeed it

151

was almost impossible to get around the streets for the military traffic, and when Hari at last made his way to Moon Lily's little house, he found it empty and in ruins.

"Alas," he said to Sam, "what can have happened to her? That wily Hakim must have taken all her money and she has been driven even from their tiny house." Hari made his way back brokenhearted toward the airfield. But on the way he passed a square which he had not seen before, and in its center there was a noble building of gleaming white stone and stainless steel and great quantities of glass. Both the building and the square were new and on the façade of the building in most elegant lettering were the words:

"Pacification Headquarters. BAPN."

While he was staring at this elegant and unscarred building, a magnificent limousine swept, sleek as a cat, to the door, escorted by six police on motorcycles. One leaped off his machine, hurried to the door of the limousine, and opened it. Out came a wizened and bent man who leaned for support on a staff of ivory cunningly encrusted with emerald, rubies and blue diamonds.

"Hakim," cried Hari. "Hakim, you villain. What have you done with Moon Lily and little Tatita and the baby? Scoundrel! Where are they?" He was about to fling himself on Hakim but Sam and one of the policemen detained him.

Hakim turned and fixed Hari with a glittering eye. "Ah, my friend Hari, the elephant boy," he cried. "I am delighted to see you." He embraced the astonished Hari and conducted him and Sam into the building.

152

Here they found a lobby of imperial elegance, the floor covered by the most expensive carpets, the walls paneled with exquisite woods. Hakim, attended by flunkeys on all sides, conducted them to an elevator which would have made a theater box for the most fastidious of monarchs, and then to an upper floor and an office of such style and luxury as to disgrace a French cardinal of the seventeenth century.

"What is the meaning of all this?" cried Hari when they were alone. "When I left you, you were a miserable man glad to have a few bowls of rice a day, and now you live in luxury beyond all imagination. How has this miracle been wrought?"

"I owe all to glorious peace—or rather to pacification," replied Hakim. "Profitable as war was for me until betrayed, peace—or rather pacification—has proved even more profitable. My dear friend, do you realize that there are now ten times more soldiers, more administrators, more civilian workers, more arms, more supplies, more stores, of all kinds in Sasia than during the late war?

"Ah, how I lamented the coming of peace! And how wrong I was! The ravages of war are now being redressed at ten times the cost of producing them in the first instance. And I, as an expert on stores and the dispatch, receipt, warehousing, cataloguing, preserving, insuring, discovering and checking of stores of all kinds, reap now ten times what I reaped before. In wartime, it cost twenty dollars to get two cans of spaghetti to any one of those heroic fellows fighting for democracy in the rank jungles of Sasia. In peace, it costs two hundred to get the same two cans of spaghetti to the survivors of that heroic struggle.

"The cost of every shellhole, in terms of explosives alone and not counting their delivery by airplane or the feeding and clothing of the pilot and his plane crew and the feeding, clothing and transportation of all those who serviced the plane, was five hundred dollars. That is for the bomb alone. To fill in each shellhole in terms of manpower, fuel, transportation, paperwork and telephone calls is two thousand dollars. Our surveys show that there are in this country a minimum of one hundred and twenty-seven thousand three hundred and eighty-four shellholes of the first degree which will require filling in, and this little sideline alone should net me, in the control of the necessary stores, ten million piasters, which is of course petty cash, but one who has known poverty does not sneeze at these things.

"And tell me now, is it true that the Best of All Possible Nations is to support the cause of the Yellow Hat Lamas against the Red Hat Lamas?"

"It is true indeed," said Hari.

"In my old age, Allah is good to me," said Hakim, piously bowing his head and closing his eyes. "I must go immediately to Tibet; for I understand that certain inquiries are being started into the handling of Pacification Stores here by those who wish to succeed me and no bribe can stop an inquiry which promises such a reward to those who make it."

"You are a villainous old scoundrel making your profit out of the grief and needs of others," cried Hari.

"We must all work according to our talents," said

Hakim. "For a villain to pretend honesty is the grossest deception and to that I will not stoop. But no doubt you wish to see Moon Lily and Tatita. I have them safely here." He spoke into a microphone on his desk; and in a few moments Moon Lily and her daughter Tatita and her infant brother, all clad in gowns of richest silk, embroidered with pink and black pearls and with buttons of lapis lazuli, were brought in.

"Sir," said Moon Lily, bowing to the ground before Hari, "my heart lives again to see my lord."

"Dearest Moon Lily," said Hari, "I was thinking at one time of a certain way you had of standing in the door of your little house at twilight and certain thoughts occurred to me and I believe that we ought to be married."

"Behold, the heavens fill with happiness and we poor mortals drown in the overflow," said Moon Lily, and swooned in the manner her mother had taught her.

There was one more surprise for the travelers, for the ugliest woman they had ever seen, lacking an eye and the end of her nose, now entered the room and, placing her hands together in the approved manner, bowed first to Hakim, then to Hari, then to Sam.

"You have not forgotten my noble mother, Celestial Flower?" said Moon Lily, who had now recovered from her swoon.

"How happy I am to see you, dear lady," said Hari, "for without you I am sure I would not have been beaten on my feet, hung up by my thumbs, imprisoned, sentenced to death and severely clubbed in the Best of All Possible Nations, nor would I be in a posi-

155

tion to marry your delectable daughter, Moon Lily."

"The ways of Providence are strange indeed," said Celestial Flower. "For all I sought to do when we met was knock out your gold teeth with a stone."

Chapter
Twenty-One

IT was agreed that all should return with Hari
to his little village on the banks of the tributary of the
Ganges, where Sam could find a new home, Celestial
Flower also; Hari and Moon Lily could raise their
children; and Tatita and later her brother could be
instructed by the Sadhu on those virtues which have
supported humanity through all the generations. Hakim, however, would proceed instead to Tibet, there
to assist in the organizing of the stores of war against
the Red Hats, which he believed would be entirely at
a stalemate without his particular talents.

He very quickly wound up his affairs in Sasia and
was off, first presenting his ivory walking stick, studded
with gems, to the Chief of Military Intelligence, who
was arrested a few days later for accepting this bribe
from Hakim, now denounced in absentia as the chief
of the native black-marketeers.

Back at last in his little village, Hari went first to
that stretch of the river where the bamboos whispered

in the evening winds and the sun sent its little splinters of light through the delicate leaves to dance in glittering myriads on the water. Arrived at the bank of the river, he removed all his clothing except a loincloth, prostrated himself in the direction of his Sacred City, and said, "Lord, I thank you that I have returned safely here. I hope you have heard my prayer concerning Golden Lotus but if you have not, Thy will be done for the wishes of men are often the ruin of the world."

He had hardly finished before he heard a squeal of excitement, followed immediately by another smaller squeal, and, rising, saw plunging toward him in a splash of spray Golden Lotus and, coming behind her, holding her mother's tail in her tiny trunk, a little calf no bigger than a sheep dog. Golden Lotus immediately encircled Hari with her trunk and lifted him high in the air, squealing with pleasure and rubbing him against her right ear, which was a sign of deepest affection. Then she put him down again and, reaching behind her, lifted up the little calf and held her out to Hari, who stroked her head and poured a little warm water over her right eye to her delight.

Meanwhile Sam, who had come to the river also, sat watching these things and thinking, and Tatita, who was with him, without bothering to remove her sari, rushed into the water to embrace the calf. The old Sadhu seated himself beside Sam and said, "There are many mysteries in the world which are beyond the reach of man and among them is the age of a woman. But I happen to know that Celestial Flower, who is undoubtedly the ugliest woman in the whole of India,

158

is only twenty-eight years old, is probably fertile and a very good cook."

Every day the Sadhu repeated to Sam, who had taken up his residence in the village with Celestial Flower as his housekeeper, the same mystic formula, namely "There are many mysteries in the world which are beyond the reach of man and among them is the age of a woman. But I happen to know that Celestial Flower, who is undoubtedly the ugliest woman in the whole of India, is only twenty-eight years old, is probably fertile and a very good cook."

When this had been going on for a month Sam took Celestial Flower before Hari, Moon Lily, Tatita, and the old Sadhu and said, "Do you promise me faithfully never to join the Parent-Teacher Confrontation, the Growing Girl Group, Child Psychology Action Center, the Bureau for Alert Children, the Bureau for Exceptional Children, the Women's Political Action Committee, the Women's Organization to Eliminate Sexual Dimorphism, the Women's Shopper's Bureau, the Women's Child-Mind Molding Committee, the Better Babies Bureau and the Mother's Help Institute?"

"I do," said Celestial Flower.

"Then although you are undoubtedly the ugliest woman in all India you have more to commend you as a wife than some of the best-looking women in the Best of All Possible Nations," said Sam. "I will take care of you if you will take care of me."

"Agreed," said Celestial Flower.

"Perhaps we shall have some children," said Sam.

"I await my lord as the earth awaits the rain," said Celestial Flower.

And so they were married and had fifteen children, and Hari and Moon Lily had fifteen likewise and Golden Lotus three more calves, which is a lot for an elephant, and the Sadhu, looking forward to his three hundred and seventy-fifth birthday, said, "The increase of life is the blessing of God; may his name be praised forever more."